Merry
Christmas!

Tina Ziolkowski

Dec, 1976.

Nat Harkins,
PRIVATEERSMAN

BY THE SAME AUTHOR:

Westward the Eagle

Nat Harkins,

PRIVATEERSMAN

By

FREDERICK A. LANE

Illustrated by

CLIFFORD H. SCHULE

HENRY HOLT AND COMPANY
New York

Contents

5

Nat Harkins,
PRIVATEERSMAN

CHAPTER ONE

The Blue Dragon, 1775

A COLD NORTHEASTER blew in over Boston Town. White caps speckled the harbor in the black gray dusk. The salt-laden wind whined through the swaying masts and rigging of the British troop transports and men-of-war which tugged at their anchor cables beyond the Long Wharf. Snarling across the fat little peninsula upon which Boston Town was built, the wind cunningly found tiny cracks and crevices in even the solidly constructed Blue Dragon Tavern in Milk Street.

Nat Harkins, working in the tavern's pantry, shivered in a sudden draft. Moving a few feet further along his bench, the boy went on with his task of peeling potatoes.

The rising rumble of voices from the dining room signified that the Blue Dragon's regular patrons were beginning to arrive. The boy frowned as he thought of them—the British officers, the Crown officials, and the prosperous Tories who met nightly at the tavern's hearth.

Nat didn't like working in a place favored by Redcoats and Tories, but, with thousands of unemployed in beleaguered Boston, he had no choice. "And," his peppery Aunt Abigail had said, "I don't want to hear any complaints out of you, young man. If it weren't that Caleb Wickerby had been shipmates with your father, you wouldn't have any work at all. Besides——"

Besides, the tavern-keeper was no Tory. If he had not lost a leg in the French and Indian Wars, Caleb Wickerby would have been polishing a musket, as patriots were doing all over Massachusetts and the other colonies. "I can't fight, lad," Caleb would say with a sigh, "so, the next best thing is to keep my lips buttoned and my ears pinned back in this tavern o' mine. The lobsterbacks and the Tories do lots of spoutin' and, sometimes, I pick up some right useful information."

Nat reached for a potato which was slimy with rot on one end. What miserable-looking vegetables, he thought. Not so long ago potatoes like these wouldn't even be fed to Boston hogs or chickens. But now, with the town surrounded by the army commanded by General Washington, precious few vegetables of any kind could be had.

As for hogs—well, it was a rare sight these days to see a porker snuffling alley refuse. And chickens seemed to have vanished completely. It had been months since Nat had been awakened by the crow of a rooster at dawn.

Finishing with the potatoes, Nat was starting on some mushy onions when he heard the clump of the landlord's wooden leg and cane on the stairway.

"Easy does it on them vegetables, Nat," Caleb Wickerby rumbled when he glanced down at the slop bucket. "You're trimmin' away too much of 'em."

"They're pretty bad, sir," Nat explained. "The worst lot we've had yet."

"True enough, lad, but"— the tavern keeper chuckled—"in one of Duff's stews, who's to know the difference?"

Nat grinned. Duff, the tavern's cook, hailed from the Sugar Islands. Probably, it was there that he had learned what certain spices could do for otherwise unpalatable victuals. The landlord had said more than once that Duff could make the King's men smack their lips over boiled harness leather, and Nat didn't doubt it one bit.

Leaning down over his knobby cane, the landlord whispered, "I've a spot of good news, Nat——"

"Is it about Jeremy?" Nat interrupted eagerly.

"No, t'ain't that, I'm sorry to say. Ain't heard a whisper about that brother o' yours since he was took prisoner last June at Breed's Hill. I reckon Jeremy's been shipped to a prison ship in Halifax——"

"Or maybe he's been taken to England to stand trial for treason . . ."

"Now, lad, don't you worry about him. He's tougher'n a pineknot and smarter'n a fox—" Caleb Wickerby broke off as a voice rang out in the dining room. "That's General William Howe a-bellowin'. I'll have to go welcome him just like I was a real Tory. Be back later to tell you that news, Nat."

As the landlord clumped off to greet the commander of the British forces in Boston, Nat's thoughts turned to his brother Jeremy. Although he loved his Aunt Abigail who had looked after him since his father was lost at sea and his mother had died, it was Jeremy for whom he cared most in all the world. Whenever Jeremy had been home from a sea voyage, they had spent every moment together.

To Nat it seemed just like yesterday when they had sailed among the islands off Boston in a little skiff which he'd made. He could almost see his older brother's handsome face aglow with a carefree smile as, with their fishing lines set, they lazed in a sheltered cove. Yet nearly a year and a half had gone by since that day when Jeremy had said admiringly:

"This is a fine little skiff, Nat. Someday you'll design a crack merchantman and I'll be her skipper."

"Someday, you'll be a skipper, Jeremy, but—it's not likely my dream will come true. Hardly any ships are being built——"

That was when Jeremy's eyes had blazed. "It's because of all the laws that have been made in England. But, mark my words—we'll have free trade again, one of these days. You're only twelve now, Nat, so you don't know how it used to be. You hadn't even been born when King George the Third got aboard the English throne fifteen years back. That thick-headed tyrant who's put his blessing on the Importation Act and——

"Why, Jeremy! You sound just like Samuel Adams! People say that someday he'll be hung for treason!"

As if unaware of the interruption, Jeremy had gone on: "Crown officials were given the right to search even private homes!" He spoke heatedly of the tyrannical laws and unjust taxes, and: "When the King's officers couldn't enforce the laws, His Royal Majesty ordered General

Gage and his lobsterbacks to come down from Halifax and make us obey at the points of their bayonets and—Well, you saw what happened, Nat."

Nat nodded. He had been on the fringe of a jeering crowd that was tossing muddy snowballs at a company of British officers who had just arrived in Boston. Suddenly someone shouted an order to fire. It might have been the exasperated officer in charge. Still, it may have been one of the townspeople eager to see an even larger salvo of snowballs. Nat never did learn whose shout it was that caused the soldiers to turn their muskets on the crowd. Three citizens were killed and others were wounded. Paul Revere, the silversmith, made an engraving of the scene which sold everywhere for eightpence a copy. The angry Bostonians armed themselves and stormed through the streets demanding that the soldiers be sent away.

"There'd have been a lot of trouble," Nat said, "if Governor Hutchinson hadn't ordered the soldiers sent over to the fort on Castle Island."

"The governor has only postponed trouble. The coals of independence are smoldering and they're going to break into flame before long. The Boston Tea Party was proof enough of that." Jeremy smiled one-sidedly.

Although Jeremy had never said so, Nat was sure that his brother had been one of the fifty or so citizens who, disguised as Indians, had boarded some British tea ships.

"That really got King George mad," Nat said. "Folks are saying that's why Parliament passed even worse laws——"

"Including the Boston Port Bill." Jeremy's eyes blazed. "The King is determined to subdue the rebellious Bostonians and make them respect the throne. This Port Bill demands a payment of thirty thousand pounds for that tea which was dumped into the sea. Until it's paid, Boston can't have any seagoing trade."

"But, it's not going to be paid, is it?" Nat asked.

"No! It won't be paid—ever! And, if the Port Bill is enforced, it will open the eyes of every red-blooded man from Maine to Georgia. Everyone will see that the King regards the colonists as cringing slaves, unworthy of decent treatment."

Now, as he peeled potatoes in the Blue Dragon Tavern, Nat Harkins thought of the long, hard months which had just passed. The people of Boston, cut off from sea trade by the Port Bill, had been on the verge of starvation. Their anger had exploded into armed rebellion at Lexington, Concord, and Breed's Hill.

Breed's Hill—that was where Jeremy had been captured by the British. Nat was thinking about the strange, terrible battle when Caleb Wickerby returned. The tavern-keeper said with a grin, "General Howe's fumin' about a supply ship that's long overdue from England. He suspects Cap'n Broughton of the *Hannah* picked her off at sea."

The boy smiled too. The *Hannah* was one of the ships of General George Washington's tiny navy. Not so long ago Nat had listened to the Britishers' scoffing comments:

"Just another small coastal schooner manned by ignorant fishermen!"

And: "Impossible that a craft like the *Hannah* could interfere with British shipping!"

"They're singing another tune now, Nat," Caleb

Wickerby went on. "But, that ain't the news I aim to tell you about." He tapped at his coat pocket. "Just got a copy of an act passed by the Massachusetts General Court. Eph Summers snuck in with it—that fellow is half-eel and half-flea!"

Eph Summers was one of Caleb Wickerby's trusted couriers. Regularly he carried information from the tavern to General Washington's headquarters.

"Accordin' to this Act," Wickerby said, "we got the right to fit out armed vessels and set up Prize Courts to try and condemn all vessels infesting our seacoast."

"That means——"

"It means that Massachusetts is goin' to issue letters of marque, Nat. These are official papers that'll give private vessels the right to grab British ships on the high seas."

Nat looked thoughtful. "Then, this Act makes everything legal. The British won't consider it piracy."

"Well"—Caleb Wickerby pursed his lips—"I wouldn't say that, lad. It so happens that the King and Parliament don't recognize our Massachusetts provincial government or the Continental Congress either. Likely, if any of our privateers get caught, they'll get into real trouble. Still," he sighed, "if only I had two good legs, I'd be aboard a privateer myself, helpin' to twist the British Lion's tail."

"You're doing mighty important work for General Washington right here, sir."

The landlord grunted. Unhooking an iron key from his belt, he passed it over to the boy. "Hustle in a few sticks of firewood for the upstairs guest rooms. And fetch in a half-dozen"—he grinned one-sidedly—"a half-dozen of them chickens from the shed. And, mind you, be sure to lock the door afterward, or them hoodlums who call 'emselves Liberty Boys will clean us out."

Ducking out through the rear door, Nat hunched himself against the bitter wind and ran to the lean-to next to the stables. As he gathered an armload of sawn-and-split fence posts, he smiled slightly. Caleb Wickerby certainly had a system for getting firewood in besieged Boston. More than one Tory no longer had a fence around his home.

He darted a glance at the screened cooler. Between slabs of salted codfish and some chunks of meat there were a couple of dozen scrawny-looking plucked fowl. Even with their legs and heads cut off, Nat knew they weren't chickens. He was pretty sure that the grayish-looking birds had but recently been letting out shrill squawks over the harbor. Still, Duff could do wonders with a sea gull.

The meat in the cooler, however, was something else again. Nat didn't think that even a genius like the Blue Dragon's cook would be able to make a very tasty dish out of a bony nag that had finally died of old age.

It took three trips to the woodshed to supply the guest rooms with firewood. Nat then delivered the so-called chickens to the cook and went back to paring vegetables until it was time for him to attend to his nightly chores. After he lit the tallow candles and whale-oil lamps, he put on a clean apron and prepared to serve the diners.

"Nat," the cook said as he ladled out a steaming bowl of fish-head chowder, "this here's for that dandified

16

colonel over by the no'th window. And—see who's just come in to set beside him!"

Nat looked out into the dining room. Sitting next to the colonel was a burly, moon-faced man. "Seth Cuffey," Nat murmured.

"Now, you watch out for Cuffey," Duff warned. "He's still awful mad at your brother for knocking the tar out of him for looting when they was both Liberty Boys, and——"

"He's still angry, all right," Nat said. "Every time he comes in here he taunts me. He tries to make me say something that could get me into trouble, but I've learned how to keep my mouth shut."

"Maybe so," Duff muttered. "But, watch out anyhow. That Seth Cuffey is slick and—he's meaner'n a wharf rat."

"He's plain no-good," Nat said, remembering how Seth Cuffey had joined the Sons of Liberty—not because he was a patriot but because he was a bully. Along with some of his cronies Seth had terrorized Tory and Loyalist families and looted their homes. But, now, he was thick as molasses with the British because he'd decided they had more than enough ships, soldiers, and guns to put down any kind of rebellion.

The air was blue with smoke from scores of long-stemmed clay pipes when Nat stepped into the dining room. As he threaded his way past the tables, he heard snatches of conversation from the smartly uniformed officers of the various regiments quartered in Boston. One voice rang out:

"I predict they'll both be caught and, when they are, both Sam Adams and John Hancock will be hanged as traitors to the Crown!"

An artillery lieutenant leaned back in his chair. Hooking his thumbs under the blue lapels of his scarlet coat, he said, "Blast me if I can understand why we haven't marched out and shriveled those rebels who've joined that tobacco farmer named Washington——"

" 'Pon my word, leftenant," a dashing dragoon officer broke in, "it appears you have not heard about Falmouth."

"Falmouth? What about that rebel town?"

"The news came today. Captain Mowatt went in there with his squadron and leveled the place. Bombarded it all day long with his guns and put the torch to what was left!"

"That's more like it!" another officer exclaimed. "That shows how we can cope with a handful of codfish eaters armed with duck guns. As soon as the weather warms a bit, we'll ride out and give Farmer Washington a proper spanking—and this silly business will be over with."

Nat smiled to himself. From the latest reports—via Caleb Wickerby's couriers—the "handful of codfish eaters" had grown to more than ten thousand men under General Washington.

As Nat approached the table by the north window, Seth Cuffey looked up from under hooded eyes. With an oddly sly smile he leaned closer to the British colonel. "That boy is certainly taking his time, isn't he?"

The colonel paused in the act of flicking an imaginary

speck of dust from the gold braid of his handsome uniform. Glancing toward Nat, he exclaimed, "Stab me,
boy, but you're slow! Hurry along with that chowder.
My gizzard's colder than the middle of an iceberg."

Nat quickened his pace. He was within inches of the
table when suddenly he stumbled. In a flash he realized
what had happened: Seth Cuffey had put out his foot to
trip him—deliberately!

The bowl went flying out of Nat's hands and the elegantly attired British colonel was drenched with fish-
head chowder.

Springing to his feet, the officer roared, "Stupid lout!

Clumsy imbecile!" He grabbed Nat by the collar, lifting him clear off the floor with one hand and slapping him hard with the other.

Nat managed to break away. "Sir," he said, trying to keep his voice steady, "it wasn't my fault. Seth Cuffey tripped me. On purpose too."

Cuffey, wiping the mess from the colonel's uniform, said indignantly: "Hear that, colonel! Isn't it just like a rebel to blame someone else for what's his own fault? Just as they blame the King for everything that goes wrong——"

"What's all this?" Caleb Wickerby hurriedly hobbled up, thrusting himself between Nat and the infuriated Britisher. His shrewd eyes took in the situation at a glance and he said soothingly, "I'm sorry about this, colonel. However, accidents do happen and——"

"I don't think it was an accident, Wickerby," Cuffey said smoothly. "Haven't you heard tell that the Harkins boys hate the British? Jeremy Harkins was took at Breed's Hill, wasn't he?"

"A rebel eh?" The colonel's jaws tensed. "By gad, I'll call the guard. I'll have him in irons——"

"Now, now," the tavern-keeper said hastily. "T'ain't no call to do that. You can see he's only a lad. Now, I'll arrange to have your uniform cleaned and I'll bring you fresh chowder myself—compliments of the house."

"You'll do more than that," the officer declared. "You'll get rid of this young rascal! If I see him in this tavern again, I'll have him jailed. Not only that, but I'll have you arrested for harboring a rebel. Is that clear?"

Caleb Wickerby swallowed. "Yes, colonel." He took

Nat's arm and led him out to the pantry. "Lad, it appears that mealy-mouth turncoat has finally got even——"

"If only I were a little bigger, I would . . ." Nat's eyes blazed.

"You'll grow, Nat," Caleb Wickerby said drily. "But, in the meantime, this is a sorry mess. I'm a-feared you'll have to stay away from here."

"I understand, sir." There was a worried note in the boy's voice.

The old tavern-keeper put his hand on Nat's shoulder. "There's nothing to worry about, lad. You come around to the back door, mornings. I reckon I can spare some provisions for your Aunt Abigail."

CHAPTER TWO

The Sign of the Spyglass

N AT HARKINS barely noticed the bitter chill in the air as he strode up Milk Street toward home. He thought bitterly: Plague take Seth Cuffey and his kind! By Jupiter, if only Aunt Abigail would give her consent, he would slip out of Boston, somehow, and join the patriots under General Washington. Or maybe he might even get himself a berth in a privateer.

Reaching the heights of Hanover Street near Cold Lane, Nat hesitated before entering the two-story Harkins' house. With Jeremy gone, Nat considered himself the head of the family. He hated to go in and tell his aunt about losing his job in the tavern. Times were so hard and every penny was needed!

He stared out over the rooftops toward the harbor that was silver-streaked with starlight. Swaying clusters of orange lights betrayed the presence of the King's ships anchored beyond the Long Wharf. In the town itself few lights flickered. Folks were conserving their tallow candles and whale oil—if they had any.

To the south, out on Boston Neck, a campfire glowed redly. The British, guarding the narrow land approach to Boston may have found some driftwood or more likely had torn down somebody's shed.

Nat's glance veered toward Gallup's Wharf by Fish Street. He saw a faint gleam and it occurred to him it might be coming from the rear window of The Sign of the Spyglass—old Isaiah Nixon's nautical instrument shop. Like Caleb Wickerby, Mr. Nixon had been a long-time friend of Nat's father. The boy had spent many pleasant hours in the shop looking over charts and sea books, sextants and chronometers.

A sudden thought flashed into the boy's mind: Isaiah Nixon just might know where work could be found. Why, there might even be some chores to be done in his shop! Then and there Nat decided that he would see Mr. Nixon that very night. At least, he thought, a visit to The Sign of the Spyglass was worth a try before telling Aunt Abigail about his bad luck.

He was about to turn away from the house when he heard his aunt's voice: "Home early, aren't you, Nat?"

Abigail Harkins was standing in the front door, a small figure in a calico blouse, homespun brown skirt, and spotless apron. "Hurry up! Don't let all that cold air in!"

Wordlessly he followed her to the wide hearth. It wasn't until then that he realized how chilled he was. His hands were numb. Rubbing them together, he hunched down by the fireplace.

"Is anything wrong, Nat?" She began stirring the contents of an iron pot which hung from a crane fas-

23

tened to the fireplace bricks. Swinging the pot back over the glowing fire, she turned to peer at the boy.

He stared into the dancing flames. It wouldn't do to look squarely at Aunt Abigail. She could see right through your eyes as if they were windows and read what was on your mind. Better not lie to her either; she would be sure to catch you at that game and then you would think you had stepped into a hornet's nest.

"Turn around, Nat," she said softly.

Reluctantly he did so. "Cold night, isn't it? A bad nor'easter——" There was just a chance that he could change the subject.

"Never mind the weather. I suspect that something is wrong."

Nat's nose told him there was codfish boiling in the pot; there would be beans and bread baking in the brick oven and, perhaps, an apple pie. However, in a last-minute effort to avoid breaking the news, he said, "What are you having for supper, Aunty?"

Abigail Harkins put her hands on her hips. "Nat, a blind loon could tell you're holding something back. For one thing, you're home early. And your jaw's hanging lower than a pelican's beak stuffed with smelt. Now, out with it!"

Nat sighed. He might have known there was no use in trying to fool Aunt Abigail. Gazing into the fire, he told her what had happened at the Blue Dragon.

When he had finished, she took a long breath. "H'm. Seth Cuffey, eh? That buffleheaded turncoat! Well, as Poor Richard says, 'Tricks and treachery are the practice of fools who haven't wit enough to be honest.'"

24

She was, Nat knew, quoting from *Poor Richard's Almanack* which had been printed in Philadelphia by Benjamin Franklin. Aunt Abigail had known Ben Franklin when he was a young lad working as an apprentice in a printer's shop near Boston's Dock Square. Now, Mr. Franklin was a member of the Continental Congress.

Nat straightened up and did his best to sound confident. "I'll find work somewhere. If I don't, well—maybe, I can . . ." His voice trailed off.

"Maybe you'll what?" his aunt demanded.

"I—I was thinking I might——"

"Join the patriots, I reckon. I might've known it, you being a Harkins. But"—she shook her head—"as Poor Richard said, 'Little boats should keep close to shore.' "

"But, Aunty," Nat protested, "some of the minutemen who drove back the British regulars from Concord and who fought at Breed's Hill weren't any older than I. Another thing, now that I'm thirteen years old, I could get to be a cabin boy on a ship——"

"What ship?" his aunt asked.

Nat told her about the Massachusetts General Court having authorized private vessels to attack all British shipping on the high seas. "These privateers," he went on eagerly, "will be needing crews. I'm sure I'd be taken on as a cabin boy or powder monkey—maybe even as a seaman. As a privateersman, I'd receive prize money. I could send it to you, and——"

"No!" his aunt said emphatically. Not yet, anyway, she thought as she turned aside. Nat was all she had left now.

After supper, Nat brought in wood from the shed, filled the water hogshead, and scoured the pots. He worked swiftly, anxious to be on his way to The Sign of the Spyglass. Watching him thoughtfully, his aunt said:

"Why not wait until tomorrow, Nat? It's getting late—" She stopped abruptly, realizing how concerned he was with finding another job. "Well," she went on, "since you feel you must go, promise me you'll be careful while you are out. Stay clear of the addlepated looters who are sure to be afoot. Remember what Poor Richard said: 'A mob's a monster; heads enough but no brains.'"

Nat nodded agreement. He intended to give the mobs a wide berth.

Making his way down the slope toward the wharves, Nat thought: Boston has surely changed. He could remember when the streets were teeming with people, even on nights as cold as this one. It wasn't so long since out-of-town folks would ride in over Boston Neck or come on the Charlestown ferry to attend the town meetings or to patronize the taverns and shops.

In those days the clatter of hoofs and the creak of wheels resounded over the cobbled streets. Now and again would come the raucous blast of the fish peddler's horn, followed by the cry of "Fresh cod, fresh halibut and haddock." And, from little chimney sweeps, with their brooms and blankets, there would come the piping call: "Sweep o' sweep——"

But, what Nat remembered most vividly was the tap of hammers and the snore of saws that came from the shipyards. His nose wrinkled with pleasure as he recalled the mingled smells along the wharves: tar and hemp, whale oil and fish, molasses, spices, and lemons from the Sugar Islands.

All that was gone now. The only ships in the harbor were the grim-looking British men-of-war, troop transports, and their supply vessels. The shipyards were silent. The streets, except for squads of soldiers and gangs of hoodlums, were almost deserted. An aura of gloom and fear hung over Boston Town.

When Nat turned out of an alley into Fish Street, he heard the distant clop-clop of an ax. Another tree being felled for firewood. He reflected that, at this rate, there wouldn't be a poplar, elm, maple—or even a fruit tree—left in Boston when this winter came to an end.

Isaiah Nixon's place of business was wedged in between a printing shop and that of a candle-maker. Both these establishments were dark, their proprietors having run off from Boston to join the minutemen. However, a flicker of light from the rear of The Sign of the Spyglass told Nat that Isaiah Nixon was in his back room.

As the boy approached the brass telescope fastened over the door, a burly roundsman emerged from the darkness, his horn lantern glowing dully. Squinting at Nat, the night watch went on bawling loudly: "A half-past seven o'clock and a cold nor'easter."

Nat rapped with the brass knocker and, a few seconds later, heard footsteps inside the shop. Then, a latch and chain rattled and the door opened a few inches.

"Nat. Nat Harkins!" a creaky voice welcomed him. The door swung wide. "Come in, lad."

When Nat entered, the old man bolted the door, then

led the way to the rear room where a cheerful crackling came from a small fireplace.

"Sit down, Nat, and warm yourself by the fire." Isaiah Nixon drew up a bench. He was a small, frail old man with twinkling blue eyes and pink cheeks. His silver hair was drawn back over his head and tied in back with a black ribbon.

A large orange cat, curled by the fire, rose and stretched. Mewing loudly, it pattered toward the rear door.

"No, no, Methuselah," Isaiah Nixon said firmly. "You can't go out prowling." He glanced at the boy. "If I let Methuselah out tonight, he'd be in someone's pot by morning."

"I know," Nat said. "Cats are bringing five shillings now. People are paying two shillings for rats."

"These are mighty hard times." Isaiah Nixon sighed. "It's fortunate you have a job at the Blue Dragon where Caleb can see to it you get some provisions——"

"I'm not working there any longer, Mr. Nixon." Nat described what had happened.

Isaiah Nixon pulled at his ear thoughtfully. "I'm not doing very much business these days—just repairing a few timepieces. Still, I think I can manage to find a few chores and errands for you——" He broke off. "I think I hear someone shouting——"

Nat, too, had heard the yells.

"The hoodlums are out again!" Isaiah Nixon rose and blew out the tallow candles on the fireplace mantle. "They've let me alone so far, but there's no sense in asking for trouble. If they see a light, they might decide to break in."

The old man and the boy sat in the half-darkness. Isaiah Nixon said, "Don't think they can see the glow from the fire——"

Nat put his head to one side and listened to the stomping of feet. "They seem to be going right past——" He broke off. Somebody had begun pounding on the front door. A raucous voice bellowed:

"I tell you I saw a glim in there, Lem. Probably old Nixon doused it and he's in there, layin' doggo."

"Come on, Toby!" another voice urged. "The old codger hasn't got anything worth takin' anyway."

"He must have! He's been fixin' watches an' clocks, ain't he? Wouldn't surprise me none if he had a flock of gold sovereigns hid behind his fireplace bricks. 'Sides, them sextants and chronometers and the like, might be worth a few shillings——"

Other voices clamored agreement and the pounding on the door started up again, accompanied by the demand: "Open up, in there. Open up in the name of the Liberty Boys before we bust in——"

Isaiah Nixon stood up and reached for a musket and powder horn racked near the fireplace. "Nat," he said, "you'd better slip out the back door and head for home."

"No, sir." Nat had gone over to the woodbox. Selecting a hefty stick, he said firmly, "I'm staying right here to help you."

CHAPTER THREE

Israel Boone

THE THUMPING on the door continued until there
came an impatient shout: "Come on, boys! Put
your shoulders to it. All together, now." There was a
splintering crash as the door was forced open and the
mob rushed into the shop.

"Stand back." Isaiah Nixon aimed his musket at the
fox-faced leader of the crowd. "Stand back or I'll
shoot!"

The hoodlums' leader put down the lantern he was
carrying. "Defyin' the Sons of Liberty, be ye, Nixon?"
He laughed harshly. "I reckon that makes you a Tory,
right enough." He turned toward Nat. "Young Harkins,
eh? You must be one of 'em, too—standin' up for a
King-lover."

"I'm no Tory and you know it," Nat declared. "And
Mr. Nixon isn't either—not any more than you're real
Sons of Liberty. The true patriots have left Boston to
join General Washington." He broke off at the sound
of footsteps behind him. Turning, he saw more ruffians
streaming in through the back door.

Isaiah Nixon had no chance to use his musket. A red-faced young rowdy dealt the old man a wicked blow which sent him headlong to the floor. Nat began striking out with his stick trying to defend himself. He heard anguished howls and had the satisfaction of knowing that his stick had landed on more than one head. A few seconds later a heavy fist caught him behind the ear and he went sprawling toward the hearth.

For a while Nat lay dazed, hardly hearing the wild yells as the hoodlums stripped the shelves and stuffed their sacks with whatever they could find. It was a piercing yowl from the orange cat which roused him. Someone had kicked Methuselah.

The boy struggled to his feet. From the corner of his eye he glimpsed a huge figure looming up in the doorway. For a second he thought that another looter was joining the crowd. Then, the big man let out a full-throated roar and plunged among the ruffians like a shark cutting through a school of herring, scattering them in all directions with his great fists.

The mob, finally realizing that a formidable enemy was in their midst, rallied. Brandishing chairs and clubs, they converged on the giantlike stranger.

By then Nat had found his stick again. He struck out at the fox-faced leader who, armed with a poker, was sneaking up behind the big man.

"Thank ye, lad—" the giant boomed. He picked up his would-be assailant by the scruff of his neck and tossed him into the midst of his followers.

The mob, having had more than enough, began beating a disordered retreat. As the last of them sped out of the front door in terrified panic, the big man laughed. "Watch those rats run, lad. They don't like having to do business with anyone except poor old defenseless men, helpless women and children. They—" He stopped. Putting his head to one side, he muttered, "Somebody's coming. Sounds like the lobsterbacks on the double. We'll have to get out of here. Likely they've been attracted by the ruckus, and if they find us in the shop, they'll accuse of us looting and clap us in jail."

"But—what about Mr. Nixon, sir?" Nat hurried back to the old man and knelt by his side. "He's hurt badly, I think."

"Well, if we leave Isaiah here those lobsterbacks are sure to put him in that pesthole of theirs they call a hospital. Still, we ain't got much choice——"

"If we could take him to my aunt's house, she'd care for him. If only we had some way of getting him there . . ."

"That's simple enough." The frail figure was scooped up in the great arms. Striding toward the rear door with his limp burden, the big man called back over his shoulder, "Come along, lad. There's no time to lose!"

Nor was there. Nat could hear voices outside the shop. But his eyes were fixed on a high shelf where the orange cat was crouched. "Just a moment, sir," the boy said, climbing up on a bench. "We can't leave Methuselah——"

"Guess you're right, lad. That critter means a lot to old Isaiah, but—hurry!"

Precious seconds passed before Nat had the trembling cat in his arms. By then the soldiers were entering The

Sign of the Spyglass. As Nat darted out of the rear door, he heard a familiar voice shouting: "There they go, men —out the back. And one of them is that same blasted rebel who dumped chowder on me in the tavern! After 'em, men!"

The big stranger was as speedy as he was strong. It was all that Nat could do to keep up with him as they zigzagged through waterfront alleys and dodged through fence gaps. Still, had it not been for the inky darkness of the night, they might not have been able to elude their pursuers.

"They're no longer right on our heels," Nat panted as his companion paused near a brick wall surrounding a tannery.

"True enough, lad, but—" He cocked his head in a listening attitude. "Sounds like they're fannin' out. They're spreadin' a net, hopin' to bag us like a school of codfish. Best thing to do is to anchor here for a spell." Gently he lowered Isaiah Nixon to the ground. "That's a bad bruise on his head, lad, but I reckon he'll be all right after a while."

The old instrument-maker groaned and asked hoarsely, "Where am I?"

"In an alley off King Street, mate."

"Israel! Israel Boone! What are you doing in Boston?" Isaiah Nixon exclaimed weakly.

"I came up from New Bedford when I heard tell of General Washington outfitting some ships out of Beverly. Calculated to find me a berth on one of 'em. On the way I decided to sneak into Boston to see my old friend Isaiah . . ."

33

Isaiah Nixon interrupted, "The boy, Israel? Is young Harkins safe?"

"Safe and sound," Israel Boone assured him. Then: "Harkins? Could the lad be Cap'n Harkins' boy?"

"That's who he is, Israel."

"I might've knowed it from the cut of your jib, lad," Boone said, turning to Nat. "I sailed with Cap'n Sam in the Sugar Islands trade. A fine skipper, Sam was—" He broke off as Isaiah Nixon moaned. "Easy, now. We'll have you in good hands afore long. Lad, just where is your house from here?"

"Just up the hill, sir," Nat replied. "On Hanover Street."

"Good." Boone listened for a few moments to the distant shouts. "I reckon we can put about on a new course and shake off those lobsterbacks easy enough. Let's shove off."

They went on again, pausing in the shadows of a deserted house near King Street until a roundsman, lantern swinging, clomped by. Winding their way through dark alleys and footpaths, they finally came to the Harkins house on Hanover Street.

The bells of the Old North Church were chiming out the hour when they went in through the rear door and were confronted by Nat's aunt.

When she was told of what had happened, she said, "Well, I do declare, Nat! This is certainly your night for trouble." She looked up from the old instrument-maker whose cuts and bruises she was washing with warm hazel water. "Nat, bring me the laudanum from the medicine

chest. A good strong dose will send poor Mr. Nixon into a healing sleep——"

Later, as they sat before the glowing hearth, Abigail Harkins said, "I'm very grateful to you, Mr. Boone. If you hadn't come along when you did, there's no telling what those wicked roughs might have done to Nat and Mr. Nixon."

Israel Boone grinned.

Nat watched the big man straighten up after stirring the fire, his shoulder muscles rippling rather than bulging under the coarse brown shirt. Israel Boone no longer appeared to be so big now that he wasn't towering over other men. However, there could be no doubt about his size; he'd had to stoop a bit to get through the doors of the Harkins' house. Yet, he wasn't like most large men whom Nat had seen before. Boone's wedge-shaped body was perfectly proportioned. When he hitched up his leather breeches, Nat noticed how straight the powerful legs were.

The mariner from New Bedford eased himself down in a chair next to a table where a whale-oil lamp was burning brightly. A thick brush of black beard covered his face, but did not conceal the long scar which slashed down his left cheek. Nat saw that Boone, like nearly every other seaman, had his long hair drawn back and tied with a dried eelskin.

But it was the man's eyes that held Nat's interest. They were blue but ever-changing. When he had first spoken to Aunt Abigail, they were a warm and friendly blue. When he had looked down upon the injured instrument-maker, they were softly sympathetic. Now, however,

36

when he spoke of the hoodlums, they turned into a cold, iceberg blue.

"Sorry I wasn't at The Sign of the Spyglass a mite sooner, ma'am," he said in his deep, surfy voice. "It always makes me feel right good to crack them kind of noggins together. I'd like to stay a while in Boston and look up those fellers—make 'em wish they'd never been born. Howsomever"—he shook his head—"them Redcoats got a good look at me. Since I don't hanker to spend time in Boston jail, I'm a-feared we'll have to be shoving off pretty quick, ma'am."

Nat sat up straight. Israel Boone had said *we*. Did he mean that he, Nat, was to go with him?

It was plain that Aunt Abigail had come to that conclusion. Her lips began trembling and her hand started upward toward her throat.

Israel Boone went on: "I can guess how you must feel, Miss Abigail, Nat being so young and all. But if he stays here in Boston, the Redcoats will likely clap him in jail. If they don't—well, the hoodlums have it in for him too. He's between two fires in a way o' speakin'."

Nat's heart was pounding. If he were to go with Israel Boone, he'd be able to sign on in one of General Washington's ships!

His aunt sighed heavily. "I suppose you are right. I hate to lose Nat but—he would have gone, sooner or later, since he's a Harkins. You'll keep an eye on him, Mr. Boone?"

"That I will, ma'am. I'll watch over Nat like he was my own kin." He rose and walked to the front window overlooking the harbor. "Some lights movin' down

37

around King Street. Reckon they're still lookin' for us. Ma'am, I don't think Nat and I ought to wait around any longer'n we have to. The sooner we get out of Boston the better."

"Nat, you'd better pack up whatever you need," Aunt Abigail said none too steadily.

Taking a lantern, Nat ran upstairs to his room. He laid out his clothing on a blanket and when he started rolling it up, he looked wistfully at the ship models which he had made. These would have to be left behind along with the books he liked so much. There wouldn't be room for them—not even *Robinson Crusoe*. His glance lingered on a slim volume which Isaiah Nixon had given him many months before. It was a collection of sea terms and, clearly, it would be very useful. He decided he would find room for it somehow. Also, he made up his mind to take the little dictionary which had long since lost its covers.

When he came downstairs, his Aunt was handing Israel Boone a bulging sack. "I wish I had more victuals for you and Nat. But I reckon this cheese, salt beef, and johnnycake will hold you for a spell."

"Bless you, Miss Abigail." Israel Boone took a purse from his pocket. "I calc'late it'll be a long, hard winter here in Boston Town, so I'd like ye to take a few of these sovereigns——"

"Sir," she snapped, "I have my silver to barter for food and firewood."

Nat, looking at the proud little figure, knew she would have to be very hungry indeed before she would part with any of her silver. Some of it had been made by

Paul Revere, one of the finest craftsmen in the colonies.

"Off with you, now," Aunt Abigail said. "And, don't worry about Isaiah and Methuselah. I'll take good care of them. Off with you—before those Redcoats come sniffing around."

Nat leaned down and stroked the orange cat that was purring contentedly by the hearth. "You'll be hearing from me, Aunty. I'll get messages to you. Eph Summer will pass them on to Caleb Wickerby——"

"Enough of this chitchat," Aunt Abigail said crisply, leading the way down the hall. Then, abruptly, she paused and drew Nat close. He felt a lump in his throat when her tear-moistened cheek pressed against his face.

"Aunty——"

"Off with you, Nat."

He shouldered his bundle and followed Israel Boone out through the back door.

CHAPTER FOUR

Farewell to Boston Town

As THEY FURTIVELY crept along in the darkness, Nat began wondering how they would be able to get out of Boston. The harbor was full of grim warships with sentries pacing their decks. And, there could be no taking the land route to the south. The narrow, tide-washed strip, known as Boston Neck, was well guarded by the King's soldiers. There remained only the back bay which bordered Boston to the west and north—a waterway infested with British patrol boats.

Apparently guessing what was on the boy's mind, the huge mariner said softly, "Wondering how we'll get clear, Nat? Don't fret. We're leaving Boston the same way I came." Turning his back to the sea, he swung confidently westward toward the inner harbor. When they skirted lofty Beacon Hill along a crooked path, Nat realized this route would take them along the shore of Mill Pond to somewhere near Barton's Point.

Nearing a fork in the trail, Israel Boone suddenly seemed less confident than he had been a while before. "H'm," he muttered. "Somehow, I can't rightly remember if it was that way or not——"

Nat spoke up: "I know all the paths in this part of Boston, sir. If you'd tell me where you want to go."

"Of course!" Israel exclaimed. "I should've had sense enough to've made you my pilot in the first place. Lad, I want to set a course for that little cove 'twixt the old copper works and Barton's Point. Know the place?"

"Yes, sir. My brother Jeremy and I used to dig clams not far from there."

"Good! Let's crowd on some canvas and get there fast. I've got a skiff hid in the brush."

Nat took the lead, setting a fast pace through this sparsely settled portion of the Boston peninsula. Since there was less need for caution, they no longer stole along quietly. Their footsteps began thudding on the path.

Suddenly there was a rustling sound in the brush ahead.

"What's that?" Israel Boone whispered.

"Nothing to worry about," Nat answered. "Could be a fox. Might be a raccoon that's managed, so far, to escape the hungry foraging parties." Or, he thought, it might be a stray tabby or dog smart enough to give the inhabited parts of the town a wide berth.

An owl hooted as they topped a rise and came closer to the marshy shore. Riffling in the northeaster, agleam with starlight, the inner bay looked like a vast jeweled carpet. Beyond the bay, on the Massachusetts mainland, daubs of yellow light came flickering from among the trees.

"Campfires," Israel Boone said. "General Washington's advance scouts tryin' to keep themselves warm."

When they reached the shoreline, the seaman gave a

grunt of satisfaction. "Here we are, Nat." He shouldered his way among the tall reeds and, a moment or so later, began hauling out a small rowboat.

In the bottom of the boat there was a pair of oars. Nat saw they had been wrapped with rags to muffle the sound of rowing. There was also a stubby little mast and a piece of stained canvas.

"The wind will blow us across, Nat." Israel's eyes were raking the harbor in all directions. "However, I reckon we'd best wait for a spell before shovin' off. The Redcoat patrol boat is due along here any time now."

Israel proved to be right. Just after the distant churchbells of Boston had chimed, the creak of tholepins and the splash of oars indicated the approach of some small craft. Presently it appeared, barely visible in the pale glow of the lamp in its bows.

As he hunched down behind the bushes, Nat heard a voice come across the water: "Stab me, sergeant, if we ain't blinking fools to be out here on a night like this. Why, we ain't seen a dirty-shirt rebel crossing either way in a month."

"Maybe so, Sykes," someone else said, "but we might see some tonight. Those two looters Leftenant Petersham told us about might be trying to escape this way. If we catch that pair, you might get to be a corporal."

"Corporal," the first speaker said with a snort. "They could make me an admiral and I still wouldn't like this here foreign country! Wish I'd stayed in Liverpool where I belong instead of joining the blinking Royal Navy."

When the patrol boat vanished behind Barton's Point, Israel and Nat stowed their gear under the skiff's stern-sheets. Dragging the craft to the water's edge, they sloshed out into the sticky mud and pushed past the reeds. Presently Israel whispered, "Jump in, Nat. I'll do the rest."

Nat eased himself over the bows. A quick shove by Israel and the boat slipped into deeper water. The big man pulled himself over into the stern and, telling Nat to take over the oars, added, "Keep her steady while I set the mast and get this rag on her. And quiet, mind you. Noise carries over water—and the wind's against us."

"Don't worry," Nat whispered back confidently. "I can handle her." At first he had no difficulty steadying the craft against the current but, suddenly, a gust of wind came swirling over the water. Nat dipped his starboard oar deep and pulled. As he did so, the oar slipped out of the tholepin, hitting the gunwale with a clatter.

Nat cheeks felt as though they were on fire. He wondered how he could have been so clumsy. "I—I'm sorry, sir. I——"

"Never mind that. The damage is likely done now. Steady her again and be quick about it!"

While Nat did so, Israel went about his task of securing the spar and setting the small sail. Now and then he glanced back past Barton's Point. "Could be, they didn't hear that noise, Nat."

"Guess they didn't—" then the boy tensed. The lamp-glare was appearing again, indicating that the patrol

43

boat was circling back. A moment later an impatient voice rang out: "Lean on those oars, you poltroons! Do you want those dirty-shirts to get away?"

"Sir," Nat said in a panicky whisper, "if we both started rowing, we just might——"

"We got to depend on the canvas." Israel calmly kept on at his task.

The patrol boat was drawing closer and Nat was sure there could be no escaping capture now. His trembling fingers had begun relaxing on the oars when Israel whispered urgently, "All right. Pull away from the shore. Quick!"

Nat leaned against the oars and pulled with all his strength. The skiff skimmed out from the shelter of the shoreline where the stiff northeast wind took over.

A shout came from the patrol boat: "There they are! Halt, you confounded rebels, or we'll shoot!"

As Nat boated his oars, Israel yelled, "Hunker down!"

The boy ducked. Shots began spanging past his head but now the skiff was moving swiftly, outdistancing the patrol boat's oarsmen. With a deep chuckle Israel said, "They'll not be able to catch us—not even if they've got any canvas. We'll be halfway across before they get it set!"

More shots rang out but they fell far short of the skiff that, slanting with the wind, was streaking through the choppy harbor for the opposite shore.

Before long the little boat approached the wide mouth of the Charles River which, flowing down from beyond Cambridge, joined the brackish back bay waters. The trees and tall brush which grew thick along the river's

44

banks broke the force of the wind. Israel, dousing the sail and unstepping the mast, took over the oars. With a deep sigh he said, "Reckon we're safe enough now—unless some quick-triggered patriot takes us for a couple of Redcoats and starts shootin'."

Nat, peering at the dark river bank, could see no sign of life. However, he felt that unseen eyes were watching every move they made. He was prepared for the challenge which rang out when Israel, rowing out of the main channel turned up a narrow creek.

"Who goes there?" a nasal voice demanded. "Halt and make yourselves known or, by Godfrey, you'll feel a musket ball in your gizzard."

"Hold your fire, you danged chowderheads!" Israel shouted, pulling for shore. "It's me, Israel Boone, back with that boat of your'n." The skiff's bows crunched into the bank.

As Nat and Israel leaped out, hauling the boat up onto dry land, a tall man loomed up in the darkness. He came toward them, a buckskin-clad figure carrying a musket crooked in his arm. "Boone, eh?" he drawled. "Didn't expect you back so suddenlike. Who's that with you?"

Israel introduced Nat to the scout whose name was Zeb Green, a sergeant in one of the Massachusetts companies. "Sergeant," Israel went on, "I'll vouch for this lad. I sailed with his father, Cap'n Sam Harkins."

"Why, in that case, the lad must be kin to Jeremy Harkins!" the scout exclaimed.

"Yes, sir," Nat said. "He's my brother."

"Well, now, I'm surely glad to meet up with you,

46

Nat," Green said warmly. "Knew Jeremy right well, I did. Any word of him since he was took at Bunker Hill?"

"No word at all," Nat said. "But—it was at Breed's Hill that he was taken prisoner."

Zeb Green grunted. "Started out to fortify Bunker Hill, we did—but decided we could make a better stand on Breed's Hill, and that's where the battle took place. But folks have started calling it the Battle of Bunker Hill and, from the looks of things, they'll be calling it that from here on out." Turning to Israel Boone, the scout asked, "Have any trouble in Boston?"

"Some," Israel said. "Ran into a little squall with the Redcoats." He told Zeb Green what had happened.

Shaking his head, Green muttered, "Boston must be a terrible place these days. However, once General Washington starts puttin' the squeeze on 'em, those lobsterbacks won't be so cocky—or them hoodlums what pretend to be Liberty Boys, either. I reckon you fellers will want to join up pretty quick, eh?"

"The sooner the better," Israel rumbled.

"You won't have no trouble. Fact is, you'll find enlistment posters plastered on every tree 'twixt here and Cambridge. If I was you, though, I'd join up with a good Massachusetts outfit like mine. Them other colonies, like Connecticut and Vermont, f'rinstance, have got good officers, but they're mighty pinch-belly when it comes to victuals."

"Nat here, and me," Israel said, "we're aimin' to sign in one of those ships General Washington is outfitting."

"Now, why in tunket do you want to do that? Why,

I wouldn't set foot aboard one of them little hookers for all the gold in the royal tyrant's treasury! The British bulldogs will blow 'em clean out of the sea."

"They'll have to catch 'em first," Israel said drily. "Anyway, that's where we're headed."

"In that case Colonel Glover is your man." The scout broke off and hailed a short, squat man. "Clem, you take over duty here while I show these fellers to our camp."

Shouldering their packs, Israel and Nat followed Zeb Green through the woods in a westerly direction and finally came to a narrow defile where militiamen were lounging about their campfires. The scout said, "You fellers can rest up here tonight and set off for Cambridge in the morning." Then, raising his voice, he announced to the men who were stretched out by the fires, "Boys, here's a pair of idjits who crave to sign up in one of them fishing smacks and fight the royal navy." There was a general laugh followed by such remarks as: "I'd as soon stick my head into a tub o' rattlesnakes," and: "Never hankered to go swimming—not in the middle of the ocean anyhow."

Nat soon learned that most of the militiamen had been farmers. Some wore buckskins but, for the most part, they were still wearing the same clothes they had used while behind their plows. They wore long homespun shirts which, belted around the waist, hung down over their breeches. Their weapons were stacked against a nearby log: a few muskets, some fowling pieces with flaring bell-shaped muzzles, and duck guns with seven-foot barrels.

One of the militiamen lifted an iron pot from the

coals and gave Nat a generous serving of venison stew. "And, ye'll be havin' some Liberty Tea to wash it down, lad?" He handed Nat a steaming mug filled with a warming brew made from raspberry leaves.

Later, rolled up in his blanket, Nat listened to the talk around the campfire. He heard Israel saying, "I tell you, boys, this war'll have to be won at sea. We got to cut the Redcoats' supply lines!"

"Can't be done, Boone," a creaky voice argued. "Trying to lick 'em on the ocean would be like a gopher tryin' to lick a tomcat."

"That's right," someone else put in. "The only thing we can do is to smash their armies. And we can do it too. We did it at Concord, didn't we? And at Bunker Hill too."

"Yes, sir!" The creaky voice started up again. "We know how to fight—we took lessons from the Injuns. We don't act like we was on parade when we get into a skirmish! Soon as General Washington gets enough cannon and powder, we'll have them lobsterbacks beggin' for mercy!"

Israel Boone snorted. "Where'll you get your powder and shot and provisions? I'll tell you: from the sailors. Captain Broughton of the *Hannah* has grabbed off some British supply ships and . . ."

"Shucks, Boone! That's only a drop in the bar'l . . ."

"Right now, it is," Israel admitted. "But, General Washington's outfittin' a navy and privateers have been authorized . . ."

"Won't do any good, Boone. What chance will fishing boats and trading tubs have when they run up

49

against all those big men-o'-war? Why, some of those lobsterback warships are floating forts. They have two or three decks on 'em and more than seventy guns!"

As the argument went on, Nat's thoughts turned to his cherished dream. For as long as he could remember it had been his ambition to design and build fine merchant vessels. Yet, with every passing month, it had become increasingly clear that the dream could never become a reality. The British were making it plain that there would be no building or manufacturing in the New World. The colonists were to be producers of raw materials only; they were to provide only those things which would keep factory wheels spinning in Great Britain.

Drowsily tightening his blanket around him, Nat became aware that the militiamen were no longer discussing ships. Their thoughts, too, had veered to the conditions which existed in the colonies. A creaky voice was saying:

"T'ain't fair! We're expected to buy things we could make ourselves—"

Someone interrupted querulously, "Well, what's the Continental Congress lollygaggin' around for anyway? Why don't they come right out and declare for independence from the Crown?"

"They will," a mellow voice replied. "Sam Adams is down there in Philadelphia right now. So's Ben Franklin. They'll open the eyes of the die-hards. Mark my words—there will come a time when we will be a free nation. There'll be no more unjust laws made overseas and no more Crown officials to enforce them. We shall become a nation of free men—free to choose our way of life."

Free to choose our way of life—Nat repeated softly. What a magnificent goal that was! As he drifted off to sleep, the resolve was in his heart to fight for that kind of freedom until it was won.

CHAPTER FIVE

Banty Spooner

A<small>T DAWN</small> Nat and Israel started along the river road which led to Cambridge. Although the cold northeast wind had blown itself out, there was a bite in the morning air. Muddy puddles had frozen solid during the night. As the two strode along briskly, Israel glanced up at the sky where a crimson sun was filtering through a thickening pink and white cirrus. "Weather's makin', Nat. Blizzard, maybe."

Nat nodded, remembering the old saying, "Red sky in the morning, sailors take warning."

The road to Cambridge was a well-traveled thoroughfare creased with wagon-wheel ruts and pocked with the hoofmarks of horses and oxen. Even at this early hour the traffic had already started. Creaking along were ox carts laden with crates of fowl, sacks of flour, and barrels of potatoes for the outposts of General Washington's far-flung army.

Now and again Nat and Israel passed groups of militiamen who were beginning to emerge from their crude shelters—lean-tos made of boughs. The men, stamping about to warm themselves, would nod with satisfaction when they heard occasional shots in the distance. These meant that the hunters who were out might be having success and that there would be wild game for the patriot pots.

Although there was activity on the roads and at the camps, the countryside itself seemed to have been deserted. The neat little clapboard farmhouses, for the most part, seemed to have been abandoned. Smoke wisped up from only a few fireplace chimneys.

Approaching the village of Cambridge, they came upon a company of men drilling in a muddy field. Looking at them narrowly, Israel commented:

"They certainly don't look much like soldiers, do they? Not at all like them British regulars. Not one of 'em has a uniform."

"Not even the officer." Nat's eyes lingered on a tall, gaunt man who must have been the officer in charge since he was barking orders. Like the others, he wore tattered homespuns and the typical loose-hanging shirt of the farmer.

As Nat's glance ranged over the soldiers, he saw that some were boys no older than himself; others were graybeards five times or more his age. While he looked at them Nat thought that what these militiamen lacked in fine equipment was more than made up for in spirit. There was a spring to their step and a pride in their bearing that couldn't be missed. These were the kind of men who had driven the Redcoats from Concord all the way back to Boston. Later they had amazed the world with their courageous stand at Breed's Hill.

53

When the squad turned at a command, Nat saw that something had been printed on the backs of many of the patriots' shirts. The words were: *"Liberty or Death"*— and the boy knew they meant exactly what they said.

Shortly after leaving the squad behind, Nat and Israel approached a point where, beyond some tall elms, they could glimpse the church steeples of Cambridge needling skyward. Now even more drilling patriots came into view and, closer to the village, tents and lean-tos spread out as far as the eye could see.

"Ever been here before, Nat?" Israel asked as they entered the village.

"Quite a long time ago." Nat told of a visit to Harvard College. "I came here once with Aunt Abigail. She wanted me to see the College which, someday, she hoped I would attend."

"And is that your aim, lad?"

"It was. I wanted to study algebra, trigonometry, and other things that would help me to become a shipbuilder. But, now . . ." his voice trailed off.

"Don't you fret, Nat. You'll have to fight for your chance to study at Harvard, but you'll get there all right."

Nat's memory of Cambridge had been that of a quiet village with neat homes and students' rooming houses. Now it was no longer a serene spot nestling among elms and maples. It was an armed camp bustling with activity.

Tents had gone up everywhere—along the roads and on the Common. Galloping past slow-moving carts were riders seemingly bound on important missions. There was an antlike stream of militiamen teeming about the redbrick college buildings. Massachusetts Hall was a barracks. Harvard was no longer a place of learning except in the rudiments of war.

Nat paused in front of one of the enlistment posters which had been tacked to nearly every wall and fence. Printed in large letters were the words: *"Hail All Men Able in Body and Spirit . . ."*

"H'm," Israel said, pursing his lips thoughtfully, "in addition to clothing and rations, a feller who joins this regiment will get sixty dollars a year. Come along, Nat, afore you find yourself signed up for some landlubber cruise. Salt water's what we crave."

A short distance further on the big mariner halted in front of a clapboard tavern. On its door, there was a sign, the Red Rooster, and for those who could not read, a large replica of a crowing rooster, carved from wood and painted a brilliant red, hung from a swivel over the entrance.

"Let's look in here, Nat," Israel said. "For one thing, I could eat a raw coot right now. For another thing, the landlord should be able to tell us where to find Colonel Glover."

Although it was still early, there were a number of patrons in the Red Rooster. Some who had already breakfasted had taken up places around the hearth. Most, however, were still at the tables and the tantalizing aroma of frying bacon and brewing coffee filled the big, cheerful room.

Nat saw a red-faced, fat man approaching them. "And what can I do for you lads?" he asked wheezily, his sharp blue eyes looking them up and down. "Enoch Spade's the name—I'm landlord of this here ordinary."

"Well, one thing you can do for us is to give us breakfast," Israel said. "After that, we aim to join up with——"

"Join up, eh?" Enoch Spade rubbed his pudgy hands together. "You'll have a wide choice with companies here from nearly all the colonies. 'Course," he added, "you won't get into any of those crack outfits from Virginia or Pennsylvania. Those fellers all have Kentucky rifles and most of 'em can shoot the whiskers off a squirrel at two hundred yards."

"We ain't interested in dry-land fightin'," Israel said. "Colonel Glover is the man we want to see."

"Well, now, I might've known you were seafaring men. So, you want to sign in General Washington's navy, eh?"

"That we do, and right quick. Where can we find Colonel Glover?"

"Easy enough, lads. He's taken over one of those Tory houses on Brattle Street for his headquarters—same as General Washington did. But come along, now. No sense in seeing the colonel with an empty stomach. Set yourselves down and I'll have Polly bring along some victuals." His eyes narrowed. "You got money, I reckon?"

Israel produced a gold sovereign and the landlord beamed. "Well, now, nothing's too good for the patriots, I always say. Here you are, lads."

Showing them to a plank table which had been polished to a rich sheen with beeswax, the landlord shouted, "Polly! Where are you, you lazy bag of bones?"

Presently a dumpy girl in a blue apron appeared and served them with bowls of porridge, a rasher of bacon, and hot corn bread.

Nat, his appetite sharpened by the brisk walk to Cambridge, was about to start eating when a clacky, metallic voice began rasping within inches of his eardrum:

"Israel! I'll be a quiddlin' alewife if it ain't Israel Boone!"

Nat turned and saw a small, wiry man wearing a peacoat, leather breeches, and a red stocking cap.

"Banty!" Israel boomed, rising to put out his hamlike hand. He towered over the little man like a mountain over a molehill. "Why, I haven't seen you since we were in the Surinam trade. Where've you been, Banty?"

"Sailin' coastwise." The words came from the little man as if he were spitting out pebbles. "That is, I was sailin' coastwise till this ruckus blew up. What brings you to Cambridge, you big walrus?"

Israel chuckled. "I might ask you the same, Banty. Now, sit down here and have some victuals—and meet up with Nat Harkins. Lad, this little rooster is Banty Spooner, an old mate o' mine. Nat is Cap'n Sam Harkins' boy. Remember the cap'n, Banty?"

"That I do, and may his soul rest in peace." Banty put out a hand and it was all Nat could do to not wince under the ironlike grip.

Banty pulled up a chair and sat down. Pushing back some wirelike strands of carrot-colored hair that had broken loose from the knot in back of his head, he said,

"I just came down along from Beverly, Israel. Seems when you're in the army, you got to make reports to your superior officers no matter what, so——"

"Army!" Israel exclaimed. "Don't tell me a deep-water man like you signed in the army!"

"I did and I didn't," Banty replied. "Right now I happen to be a lieutenant, but that's no matter. Soon as I get to sea, I'll be a first mate—and any bufflehead who calls me any different or tries to salute will feel a belaying pin on his noggin and you can lay to that——" He broke off as the serving girl appeared, and ordered a double rasher of bacon, a pot of baked beans, corn bread, and coffee.

"I see you've not lost your appetite," Israel commented. "But what's all this about being in the army and going to sea? Out with it, Banty."

"I guess it does seem a mite queer," Banty said. "Still, a feller like me isn't happy less'n he has a live deck under him—and if joining an army is the way to do it—well, he joins. Anyway, that's what I did. I came up here about a month back with Cap'n Manley from Marblehead and I joined Colonel Glover's regiment——"

"Colonel Glover—" Israel broke in. "He's the man Nat and I are here to see, Banty. We want to sign in one of them ships he's outfittin'——"

"Why in tarnation didn't you say so?" Banty asked testily. "I could've told you I was mate—I mean, lieutenant in the *Lee*. Cap'n Manley's skipper—and we reckon to sail within a week. We expect to start grabbing off some of the Redcoats' supply ships. You fellers want to sail in the *Lee*?"

"We sure do!" Israel exclaimed. "Haven't I been tellin' you——"

"All right. All right." Banty picked up his knife and fork as the girl set down platters of food. "Soon as I get victuals into me so's I'll have some strength, I'll take you fellers over to Colonel Glover's headquarters and sign you up. We need seamen, Israel." He nodded toward Nat. "And, as for you, lad,—any kin of Cap'n Harkins ought to make a good hand. Now, if you fellers will stow the gab, I'll tackle these here rations. Can't eat and talk at the same time—and I'm weaker'n a sick jelly-fish."

CHAPTER SIX

The Schooner *Lee,* Four Guns

NAT HARKINS was aloft. From the crosstrees of the schooner *Lee* he scanned the misty pink horizons in the growing dawn as the little Continental vessel, ever on the alert for the enemy, probed the outside waters of Massachusetts Bay.

Now and then Nat flicked a glance at his fellow lookout. The tall, slender young man who was awkwardly straddling the spar and clinging tensely to the rigging seemed anything but at home aloft. It was clear even to Nat, whose seagoing experience was limited to sailing a small skiff, that young Calvin Crane was a green hand.

Nat wondered about Calvin Crane. Although the tall youth's straw mattress lay next to Nat's in the forecastle, they were hardly better acquainted now than when the cruise first began. Young Crane kept apart from his shipmates, rarely joining in their talk. Not once had Nat seen him smile. His thin face was set in a grim expression and bitterness smoldered in his gray eyes.

All that Nat knew about Crane was what he had heard from scuttlebutt gossip. According to the talk, Calvin

Crane had been a Harvard student. Also, he was learning to be a doctor.

The two were aloft because a double lookout had been ordered by Captain John Manley. The schooner's commander felt that two pairs of eyes were needed in these perilous waters.

When Banty Spooner, the mate, had ordered them up the ratlines, he had snapped, "Sing out when you see anything, lads. A sail might mean a lobsterback frigate which could make driftwood out of this packet with a single broadside. Or, it might mean a fat supply ship, which is what we're after. Keep your eyes skinned."

The morning was fairly clear except for a smudge of haze blurring the rim of the horizon. A long, rolling swell was on the sea, the aftermath of a three-day storm which had blown up soon after the *Lee* had put out from the Massachusetts port of Beverly.

Nat's eyes ranged the deck below briefly. The schooner, he mused, was surely small. Much smaller, in fact, than any of the British brigs, brigantines, and ships he had seen in Boston Harbor. He wondered how the tiny *Lee* armed only with four four-pound cannon and a few swivels, could ever expect to stand up to a larger Britisher.

A surging swell sent the *Lee* rolling over like a playful dog. Blocks and gear rattled, timbers creaked and canvas slatted as the tall foremast described a dizzying arc across the sky. Over the ship sounds Nat heard Calvin Crane's hissing, indrawn breath. Young Crane was certainly scared although he was trying not to show it.

The schooner's general direction was southward toward the tip of Cape Cod which curved out into the blue vastness of Massachusetts Bay like a great fishhook. Now, however, because of the haze, that headland was not visible.

Glancing below again, Nat saw that the *Lee* was coming alive. All hands were busily shipshaping the vessel, repairing the damage done by the recent storm. From aloft the men looked like ants as they went about their tasks of repairing broken gear, setting up loose rigging, or swabbing decks.

The sailmaker, on the forehatch, was repairing torn

canvas. Smoke, wisping from the galley stack indicated that the cook was preparing breakfast. The boatswain's whistle peeped continually.

The pale sun was shouldering up over the sea when Nat's companion broke his silence. "I—I thought I saw something," he exclaimed, pointing over the starboard bow. "Something white."

Nat peered in the direction indicated and presently saw a feathery plume rise and then subside. "A whale," he explained. "Probably a pod of sperm judging by the slanting spout."

"Oh!" was the disappointed reply, then harshly: "Why couldn't it have been a confounded Britisher we could blow to Jericho?"

Nat blinked. He hadn't expected such a violent outburst from the scholarly-looking, quiet young man.

Noticing Nat's startled look, Calvin Crane said grimly, "I—I just can't forget Falmouth."

"Falmouth! Why, that's the town——"

"It was a town. It isn't now. There's nothing left of Falmouth. Perhaps there's nothing left of my family either."

Nat was beginning to understand the reason for Calvin Crane's brooding silence. He knew what had happened. He remembered hearing the British officers in the Blue Dragon boasting about Captain Mowatt whose five warships had bombarded and burned the defenseless village.

"I—I haven't liked to talk about it," Calvin Crane said in a low voice, "but perhaps it's best if I do——"

He explained that he had been away from home, attending a Harvard class which had been transferred to Concord when hostilities broke out. When he heard of the attack on Falmouth he had hurried there to find the Crane home a mass of rubble and ashes.

"I could learn nothing of my people," he said bitterly. "They were gone. I'm hoping they may be at the farm of a cousin in the Ossipy Hills of New Hampshire." He paused, then: "I think you can understand now why I joined the patriots even if I was close to being a Loyalist."

"A Loyalist? You were a Loyalist?"

Calvin Crane nodded. "Many Harvard students felt that the differences with England could be settled peaceably. We were sure that Dr. Franklin would be able to influence the British Parliament and that the harsh laws imposed on the colonies would be repealed."

"But laws were repealed, like the Stamp Tax, and then other laws were passed which were worse."

"The Whigs repealed the Stamp Tax," Calvin Crane explained. "That was during the brief period when they controlled Parliament."

Nat frowned thoughtfully as his glance raked the sea. He was somewhat vague in his mind about the workings of the British government.

He knew, of course, that Parliament consisted of the House of Lords who represented the noblemen; and the House of Commons whose members were elected by the merchants and working people—the "commoners" as they were called. Parliament made the laws and the King was kept advised by his appointed ministers.

64

As for Whigs and Tories, Nat was aware that these made up the two important political parties in England, and that each was forever trying to get control of the Parliament.

"Whigs. Tories," he said. "What queer names."

"They're odd," Calvin Crane admitted. "I became curious about them at Harvard——"

The origin of the word "whig" he told Nat, was uncertain. "It may derive from the Scots word 'whiggam' used by the peasants when driving horses, but it also means horse or cattle thief in Scottish dialect.

" 'Tory' comes from a motto of the Irish people who were loyal to King James during the Irish Revolution. Their motto was '*Tar a Ri*' which means 'Come, oh, King.' "

Calvin Crane shrugged. "But all that's neither here nor there. Today we know that Whigs belong to the political party sympathetic to the cause of the colonies, whether they are here or in England."

"And Tories are just the opposite." Nat nodded. "They want to crush the colonies." He was silent for a while, then asked, "But why do the English people want the Tories in power. Why do they elect men who treat us so badly?"

"They don't. I've talked with visiting students from Oxford. They told me that neither the Whigs nor Tories speak for the people. Of the eight million souls in England, probably less than a third are represented in Parliament. The average commoner has no voice in his government."

Nat's forehead wrinkled. "Why then," he asked bluntly, "were you a Loyalist? Why did you want the colonies to stay under the King's rule?"

"I thought conditions would change," Calvin Crane replied. "Ever since King John was compelled to sign the Magna Carta, Englishmen have been striving for freedom. There has been one reform after another. No longer can a king order a subject hanged simply because he doesn't like the way the man ties his pigtail. In time England will know the meaning of real liberty. But we of the colonies will know it first—those of us who don't die fighting for it."

A while later when two seamen came clambering up the ratlines to take over lookout duty, Nat and Calvin Crane went below to join the starboard watch at breakfast.

As they sat on the forehatch with their rations of oatmeal, hard sea biscuits, and chocolate, Israel Boone stretched out nearby. "Well, lads," he said, "I reckon this beats tramping around in the snow and mud like foot soldiers got to do." He grinned at the seamen clustered nearby. "Don't look much like army privates, do they?"

Nat nodded. He had seen little evidence of saluting or other military regulations aboard the *Lee*.

"Cap'n Manley's a real blue-water skipper," Israel continued. "I calc'late he knows a sailor's a sailor no matter what handle you lash onto him."

All around them the crew members were talking about the *Lee's* chances of capturing a British ship and the possibilities of prize money. A red-bearded seaman named

Reddy Malone was muttering, "We won't get rich in a hurry. We ain't no privateer. Them fellers get the whole smear when they capture a ship, but we only get a third of the value of ships and cargo we grab. Not only that, with a little tub like this——"

"She's sharp, Reddy," interrupted a wizened little seaman. "And she's fast. Give this here schooner a fair wind and she'll overhaul most of them clumsy Redcoat scows."

"Maybe she will," Reddy growled. "But what happens when we catch one of 'em and she's got more guns than we have?"

Israel Boone spoke up. "I reckon Cap'n Manley knows what he's about. Likely he'll hoist a foreign flag when we sight a Britisher so we can run alongside her without her suspecting anything. Then we'll have a boarding party on her before she knows what's up."

"You mean we go aboard and fight 'em on their own deck?" a fisherman from Marblehead asked.

"That we do if need be," Israel replied. "Hand to hand with pistols and cutlasses."

The fisherman put down his empty porridge bowl. "Looks to me like some of us are going to get hurt."

"Likely," Israel said drily. "Fighting bulldogs is a mite more dangerous than catchin' codfish. Still, we ain't so bad off. If any of us get wounded we got somebody to patch us up." He nodded toward Calvin Crane. "I hear tell that young Crane here knows considerable about doctoring."

"But I'm not a doctor," the tall youth protested. "It's true that I've studied medicine, hoping to enter the profession but——"

"Don't be so modest, lad. Why, Banty Spooner was telling me that old Doc Goldthwaite in Boston had you helping him out when his rheumatics was bad. Banty says folks thought you was a fine sawbones."

When breakfast was over, gunnery practice was ordered aboard the *Lee* and Nat ran to his station at number four gun which was captained by Israel Boone. He was soon joined by the others of the gun crew, Reddy Malone and a stocky seaman named Joe Patch.

"Wal, lads," rumbled Israel when he came aft. "What with the foul weather and all we ain't had too much practice with this here little spitfire." He gazed fondly at the stubby four-pound cannon which snouted out toward a square gunport cut in the bulwarks. "So I reckon we'll just go over everything again before we do any shooting at them kegs the mate's going to toss overboard."

After Nat and the others brought up shot, matchtubs, powder, and other gear needed to man the gun, Israel went on with his instructions:

"First of all it's mighty important to see that the tackles are sound and secure. Why, when I was privateerin' in the French and Injun War I saw a nine-pounder bust away from her breechings. Ripped clear on the recoil and killed two fellers——"

"Ah, we heard all that before," Reddy Malone interrupted impatiently. "Them tackles are all right. Anybody can see that with half an eye."

"Smart, ain't you, Reddy?" Israel's eyes narrowed. "You appear to know all about layin' a gun, eh?"

"I oughter," Reddy snapped, "after listening to you

68

gab about it so much. We been over all this stuff a dozen times. I know this here pea-shooter inside out."

"You do, eh?" Israel put his hands on his hips. "I'm glad to hear that, mate. Fact is, I'd be right pleased if you'd tell the other lads here how to load and fire this piece."

"Wal, now . . ." Reddy hesitated.

"Now, now, Reddy. Don't be parsimonious with your learnin'. Come on now and share it with the others."

Reddy took a deep breath, then: "All you do is take one of them there iron balls." He pointed at the shot rack. "You shove it into the end of the gun and then you take aim and fire. That's all there is to it, although to hear you tell it, shootin' a gun is harder than skinnin' a whale."

Israel grinned. "If I was a Britisher, Reddy, I'd sure be scared to have an expert gunner like you popping away at me. That is, if you know some way to fire this here cannon without putting any powder in it."

Reddy's neck became almost as red as his beard as Israel went on: "Maybe you're the best codfisherman what ever put out o' Marblehead, but it's plain as the beak on a pelican that you don't know any more about gunnery than a cockroach. From now on keep your tongue from flapping and you might learn something."

Israel went on to explain again the precautions to be taken before firing. The powder kegs should be set to windward so that stray sparks blown by the wind wouldn't explode them.

"Sponging's important too, and that's your job, Nat. After firing you swab out that barrel until its cleaner'n a shark's tooth. Leave any burning shreds of powder in there and we might get a misfire and then we'd all be shaking hands with Mister Beelzebub."

While Israel was speaking, several kegs were thrown over the stern. The schooner pulled away and the boatswain's whistle shrilled. The *Lee* came about, booms swinging as she ran off on a new tack to bring the kegs into shooting range.

Target practice however, was to be delayed that day. Just as the crew of number one gun was hauling out to fire, a hoarse shout came from the lookout aloft:

"Sail ho! Sail ho! Off the starb'd beam!"

CHAPTER SEVEN

The Strange Brigantine

TENSION GRIPPED the Continental schooner as a tiny speck of white loomed in the haze to the west. All eyes were watching the sail which was growing swiftly. Evidently the stranger's lookouts had sighted the *Lee*, and her commander was maneuvering his vessel for a closer look.

"Since she's bearing from the west," said Israel Boone, "I reckon she's out of Boston or some other port in northern Massachusetts."

"Could be she's one of them British transports or supply ships," suggested Joe Patch, "homebound for England from Boston."

"Or a King's frigate," muttered Reddy Malone, "bristling with guns. There's several of 'em on patrol off this coast."

Still, Nat was thinking, the stranger might well prove to be friendly. Possibly she'd turn out to be one of the other schooners serving with General Washington's little fleet. Both the *Harrison* and *Warren* were known to be cruising in Massachusetts Bay.

71

Friend or enemy, Captain Manley was taking no chances. In addition to the four-pounders which had already been unlimbered for target practice, he ordered some small swivel guns manned fore and aft. Every stitch of canvas was shaken out so that the *Lee* would be ready to take advantage of the light breeze. Should the strange craft turn out to be hostile and too powerful to engage, the *Lee* would be ready to show her heels.

The mate who had gone aloft with his telescope shouted down to the captain: "She's a fore-and-after, sir. Sloop-rigged by the look of her."

Some of the tension drained out of the crew. At least the oncoming vessel wasn't a frigate or large ship-of-war. Such craft carried square sails.

The triangular patch of white grew larger by the minute. Soon Nat could see that the stranger was on a south-southeasterly course which, if maintained, would bring her across the *Lee's* bows.

Israel rumbled, "She's a sloop, right enough, Nat. Look at that spar on her. Ninety feet if it's an inch. Yankee built, she is, too."

"If she's a Yank," Reddy Malone asked, "why's she nosing around out here? Those fellers must be crazier than us, sailing in these waters in a packet that size."

"Maybe they ain't so crazy as you think, Reddy," Israel said. "Maybe—" He broke off as the sloop suddenly tacked, then ran closer on a course to take her around the *Lee's* stern.

"Jumpin' Jehosophat!" Joe Patch exclaimed admiringly. "Look at her fly. They've got real seamen aboard

72

that sloop. You don't see Britishers handlin' a craft like that."

Israel was squinting intently at the speeding stranger. "She's out of Portsmouth or Newburyport. Or, might be, Beverly. It's my guess she's a privateer."

Israel's opinion that the stranger was friendly must have been shared by Captain Manley because he soon ordered the *Lee*'s colors hoisted to the gaff. A short while later the oncoming sloop let fly her own emblem: the Pine Tree Flag of Massachusetts. Then, tacking neatly again, she came surging alongside, her crew lining the rails.

A tall man with a red bandanna tied around his head strode to the sloop's larboard rail aft and shouted:

"Ahoy the *Lee*. This here's the Massachusett's privateer *Starlight* out o' Newburyport, commissioned by the General Court. Cap'n Lemon at your service. You fellers seen anything of a lone lobsterback supply brigantine?"

"Nary a sign," Captain Manley replied through his leather speaking trumpet.

"Well, sir," the privateer captain shouted, "just before we sailed we got word that a squadron of supply vessels just arrived from England escorted by a frigate. Seems like they had trouble during that last storm. One of the supply ships—a brigantine called the *Nancy*—got separated from the others. She ain't put in an appearance and now the bulldogs are swarming out to look for her. Better keep an eye peeled for 'em, Cap'n."

"Thanks, Captain Lemon," Captain Manley answered. "I'll keep an eye out for the *Nancy*, too, just as you'll be doing."

74

"Not me," Captain Lemon boomed back. "I'm hankering to get at those fat British merchantmen in the Sugar Islands trade from England. So the *Nancy's* all yours, and good luck to ye." With that he spun around and began snapping out a series of orders. The *Starlight's* great span of canvas filled and she hauled away swiftly, squaring off on a course toward the open sea.

"Secure the guns," Captain Manley ordered. Apparently gunnery practice was to be postponed so that the *Lee* could search for the *Nancy*.

Nat watched the graceful speeding sloop for a while before turning to his tasks. He was fascinated by the craft's sleek lines and by the effortless way she sped off into the distance. He was thinking that if ever he learned the shipbuilding trade he might be able to design a sloop as fine as the *Starlight*—or one even faster, perhaps. Reddy Malone's voice interrupted his musing:

"That *Starlight* sure carries a big crew, Israel. Her decks and rigging was alive with seamen."

"She has to have 'em," Israel replied. "Ordinarily a dozen or so could handle that sloop fair weather or foul, but—when you go a-privateerin' you need plenty of extry hands. For one thing you've got the guns to man when you get into a fight. Besides, when you start capturing ships you need prize crews to put aboard 'em and take 'em into port." He turned to Nat. "Think you'd like to ship in a privateer, lad?"

Nat stole another look at the vanishing *Starlight*. "I'd like to sail in a fast sloop like that one," he said. "But is privateering right?"

"What's wrong with it?" Reddy Malone snorted. "Me,

75

I reckon to sign in a privateer soon as my hitch is over in this packet. That is, if I get a chance."

"You'll get your chance," Israel said as he lashed the canvas cover over the cannon. "Massachusetts has made privateering legal and aboveboard. Won't be long before the Continental Congress and the other colonies will be doing the same. Then you'll see privateers by the hundreds putting out from all the seaports."

Nat looked up at the big mariner with a thoughtful frown. "But I've heard people say that privateering is the same as piracy."

"It isn't, Nat," said Israel flatly. "Now, mind you, I'm not saying there wasn't plenty of greedy privateers in the French and Injun War. I reckon there'll be plenty of fellers privateering in this war, too, who are thinking only of the profits they'll get. But there'll be others who'll put patriotism way ahead of gold.

"Anyway, privateering's right necessary to get independence. We haven't got a navy. The Continental Congress is gabbing about having one and maybe sometime we'll have a fleet strong enough to lick England. But it won't be this year—or next. Might take us twenty years or maybe fifty. In the meantime we got to depend on privateers."

"But how can privateers do much good?" Joe Patch wanted to know. "They can't lick them big bulldogs."

"They'd be fools to try. But that's not their job any more'n it's our job here in the *Lee*. Merchant ships is what they're after. The more the privateers grab, the less the British have to fight us with. And all them provisions, guns, and powder—not mentioning the ships

76

themselves—will come in right handy for the colonies."

Joe Patch grunted. "The British merchants won't like losing ships and cargoes," he said dubiously. "Won't be long before they start squealing to the King and Parliament. That's when they'll get convoys. Mark my words, there'll be plenty of big bulldogs herding those merchant ships across the Atlantic to blow the privateers off the sea."

Israel grinned and his eyes lit up. "It's plain you don't know much about privateering, Joe. The privateers will hang along the trade routes and they'll cut out prizes just like a fox let loose in a chicken coop."

All that day and the next the *Lee* cruised the vast stretch of Massachusetts Bay between Capes Cod and Anne in search of the British supply vessel *Nancy*. Since Captain Manley estimated that the brigantine would have been driven northward by the storm, he ranged mostly in that area. However, no sail had been sighted.

On the afternoon of the third day Nat and Calvin Crane were on deck forward mending clothing. "Looks to me, Calvin," Nat said, "that the *Nancy* might have limped into Boston without being sighted."

"Or she may have been lost at sea. Anyway—ouch!" Calvin grimaced and sucked his thumb where the needle had pierced it. As he began sewing his ripped shirt again he said, "This seafaring life is certainly hard on clothes, Nat. Very different from my life at Harvard. There we wore out only the seats of our breeches."

"Harvard!" Nat sighed. Even if the college ever reopened at Cambridge, it wasn't likely he would ever become a student there. A college education needed money

77

and lots of it. Unless you happened to have a prosperous merchant for a father, as Calvin had, it was useless to even dream of a higher education.

"Did you want to go to Harvard, Nat?" Calvin asked.

"I've often thought about it. I'd be able to study algebra there and a shipbuilder should know algebra."

"Geometry and trigonometry too," Calvin said. "You'd learn that and more at Harvard, Nat. You'd study philosophy, astronomy, Latin, and——"

"I could do without those subjects. They wouldn't help me much in designing ships."

"They would help in designing your life, Nat," Calvin Crane said quietly. "I've never forgotten what Dr. Franklin once wrote: 'If a man empties his purse into his head, no man can take it away from him.'"

The mention of Benjamin Franklin brought a wave of homesickness to Nat. He thought of his Aunt Abigail who was so fond of quoting from *Poor Richard's Almanack*. A whole parade of memories began marching through his mind: Caleb Wickerby and Duff at the Blue Dragon, Isaiah Nixon and his orange cat, Methuselah, and—Jeremy. Where was his brother Jeremy now?

Abruptly his thoughts were broken by the lookout's ringing cry from aloft. "Sail ho! Sail ho! Starb'd bow."

Jumping to their feet, Nat and Calvin ran to the starboard bulwarks. A bank of slate-gray clouds hung over the eastern horizon and, for a while, they could see nothing. Then came a slight rift in the murk and the top-hamper of a vessel became visible.

Nat peered sharply at the stranger. "She might well be the *Nancy*, Calvin. At least she's a brigantine."

"A brigantine? How can you tell? She looks just like this schooner. Anyhow, she has two masts."

"Look close, and you'll see that she has square sails on her foremast," Nat explained. "A schooner is fore-and-aft-rigged on both masts."

Calvin, puzzled, glanced aloft. "But we have square sails forward too."

"Only topsails. Some schooners carry square-rigged topsails when they have contrary winds to worry about, but they're still called schooners." Nat couldn't quite understand why anyone who had lived so close to the sea should know so little about ship's rigs.

As if guessing Nat's thoughts, Calvin said, "I've seen vessels coming in and out of port all my life, but I guess I never looked at them closely. I never expected to go to sea and if the British hadn't burned Falmouth . . ." His eyes suddenly glinted with anger. He glanced at the brigantine again and went on in a grim voice, "If that's the *Nancy*, I wonder if we'll get a chance to board her and fight?"

"If fighting is necessary to make her surrender," Nat replied, "I expect we will."

CHAPTER EIGHT

Capture!

A s the two vessels drew closer together, Captain
Manley climbed aloft and aimed his telescope on the
brigantine. Those of the *Lee's* crew who were on duty
kept glancing away from their work to squint nervously
into the distance. The men who were off watch lined the
bulwarks and speculated about the oncoming vessel.

Nat heard Israel's rumbling voice: "We'll know soon
enough if she's an enemy. She'll fly the Union Jack."

"What makes you so sure of that, Israel?" Reddy Malone asked.

Israel snorted. "She's headed for Boston, ain't she? If
she came all the way from England how'll she know
about Continental warships like us being in these waters
waiting to pounce on her? She'll have no reason for not
showing her colors."

Reddy pulled at his beard. "She's bigger than us.
Reckon she'll be armed, Israel?"

The big seaman shrugged. "She ain't built to carry
heavy guns, but I wouldn't be surprised if she had more
armament than we got."

Joe Patch jerked nervously at his pigtail and frowned at the sea. A brisk west wind was blowing and whitecaps sparkled in the slanting rays of the afternoon sun. "H'm," he muttered. "I hope she ain't got any guns but if she has, I hope the skipper won't give her a chance to use 'em."

"He won't if he can help it," said Israel.

Presently Nat saw the distant craft tack and come about on a new course. That was when Reddy Malone exclaimed hoarsely, "Jumpin' Jehosophat! She's coming right at us. What if she's a man-o'-war?"

"She ain't." Israel gave Reddy a scornful look. "As for her heading for us—well, she has to tack to fetch Boston in this wind. I thought you were a sailor, Reddy?"

Reddy grinned sheepishly. "Reckon I'm a mite jumpy, Israel. I never done any sea fighting like you have."

Captain Manley came rapidly down the ratlines and strode aft. Seconds later the boatswain's whistle peeped and the cry: "All hands aft on the double," rang out. Footsteps thudded on the deck as the crew quickly assembled in a semicircle forward of the binnacle.

The captain flung an order to the helmsman and then faced his crew. His eyes were blazing like twin lights in his craggy sea-burned features. In a deep voice he addressed the men:

"I have every reason to believe that the brigantine yonder"—his glance veered toward the starboard bow —"is an enemy craft. The chances are good that she's the *Nancy,* laden with goods for the British army in Boston." He paused, then: "I intend to take that vessel, one way or another."

A cheer went up from the crew. "We're with you, Cap'n," somebody yelled. Another man cried, "Lead on sir. We'll grab the lobsterback ship for you in the name o' liberty."

The captain held up a hand for silence. "I'm not a man to avoid a yardarm-to-yardarm fight. You'll find that out if you serve under me long enough. However, I'd rather not sink the brigantine. If she's the *Nancy,* her cargo is important to us——"

Nudging Nat, Israel whispered. "Remember what I told you? The skipper knows what he's about. He's goin' to surprise 'em, privateer-fashion."

Captain Manley continued, "The guns will be unlimbered but the gunports will remain triced up until we're alongside the brigantine. There will be no firing without a direct order. We'll fly the Dutch colors and appear to be a friendly merchantship bound for Europe. I want to surprise the enemy."

Briefly the captain revealed other details of his plan and explained what he expected of the crew. He ordered the swivel guns manned and the four-pounders ready for action. All hands, except those engaged in handling the schooner, would be issued cutlasses or pistols.

"Although we'll be ready to fight," Captain Manley said, "I don't want the enemy to know it. All hands, except the regular working crew, will stay out of sight behind the bulwarks. If the brigantine becomes suspicious and opens fire, we will engage her with our cannon. But I'm hoping to run alongside her as close as possible, then drop our gunports. I expect she'll strike her colors, but if not——"

"If not, the *Lee* would run alongside and the grappling hooks would be thrown over. With the two vessels lashed together, a boarding party could swarm over the bulwarks onto the brigantine's deck and subdue her crew.

"Hand-to-hand fighting," muttered Reddy Malone.

His glance raking the crew, Captain Manley concluded, "Remember this, men. That vessel's cargo might mean the difference between victory and defeat for General Washington and the patriot army at Cambridge. That's all." He turned and addressed the mate: "Clear for action, Mr. Spooner."

Immediately the Continental schooner began buzzing with activity. Officers strode about, barking orders and assigning men to their various stations. The quartermasters started issuing small arms.

Nat was hefting the vicious-looking cutlass he had been given when he heard his name called. Lieutenant Ogilvy, the second officer, barked, "Boone, Malone, Patch, Harkins. Stand by number four gun and await orders. Keep out of sight. Have small arms handy. Stand ready to board the enemy——" He went on forward, bawling: "Bagsby, Epps, Crane——" His voice grew indistinct and was lost in the din.

Israel Boone's eyes were sparkling as he unlashed the canvas tarpaulin from number four. "Let's get some teeth into this little lady, lads." He ordered his gun crew to fill the shotracks and bring up the powder, slow matches, and buckets of sand from below.

A quarter of an hour later the hubbub and confusion aboard the *Lee* began to subside. The cannon were primed and loaded and the swivels ready to be mounted. The main boarding party was armed and ready to come to grips with the enemy.

Nat stared at the fast-approaching brigantine. Although she was in full view she was still too far off to see if there was any unusual activity on her decks.

Banty Spooner trotted forward, making the rounds to give the guns a last-minute inspection. "You fellers ready to engage the enemy?" he asked.

Israel gave a mock salute. "Yes, sir. We're ready, lieutenant Spooner, sir."

"Belay that," Banty growled. "And the salutes, too, you overgrown grampus, or I'll pin your ears back."

Israel chuckled. "Like old times, eh, Banty?" He nodded toward the brigantine. "You saw her through the glass. Think she'll fight?"

"She will if she suspicions us," Banty said. "But chances are we'll run right up alongside her and, if she won't strike her colors, then I'll get the boarders on her, and the rest of it'll be like shooting fish in a tub."

"You leading the boarders, Banty?" Israel asked.

"That I am." As he went forward, Banty flung back over his shoulder. "Keep your powder dry, boys."

The *Lee* settled down to the tense quietness which always precedes action. Some of the crew were on deck or aloft, attending to routine shipboard duties. When the order came, they would join the fighting men concealed behind the bulwarks.

"Maybe she won't be fooled," muttered Reddy Malone, crouched near Nat. "What if she's ready and waiting, just like we are? If she lets go a broadside we might be blown to smithereens."

Nat swallowed. The same thought had come into his mind and his heart was pounding so hard he was afraid the others might hear it.

Israel chuckled. "You look like a sick sea gull, Reddy. Reckon you'd give your left eye to be settin' codfish lines right now, eh?"

"No argument about that," Reddy admitted. "I don't know anything about this kind of fighting and, what's more, I'm not too eager to learn either. Fishing's my business. I wouldn't be here doing this kind of work if it didn't have to be done."

"I agree with Reddy," said Joe Patch. "You're a fighting fool, Israel. So's Banty and some others aboard here. But most of us would as soon be riding out a hurricane in a dory as be aboard this schooner right now. Me—well—I'm feeling as scared as Reddy looks."

Reddy looked at Nat. "What about you, lad? Got flying fish in your gullet too?"

Nat nodded and tried to grin.

A passing seaman paused saying: "That brigantine's nigh off'n the starb'd beam, boys. Won't be long now before feathers are flyin'."

Nat peered through a crevice in the gunport and was able to see the brown hull of the brigantine. Now that she was closer, signs of storm damage were visible. Ragged canvas bellied out from her makeshift tophamper and there were wide gaps where the sea had torn away portions of her bulwarks.

As the brigantine went past in the opposite direction, the boatswain's whistle shrilled and the crew aloft and on deck went about their task of bringing the *Lee* around sharply. Muffled orders lifted: "Ready, ready." "Ease down the helm."

The *Lee* leaned and heeled as the wind caught her canvas. "Spanker amidships." She was coming about, now, blocks and gear straining.

Nat was so carried away by the expert handling of the schooner that, for a while, he forgot all about the possible perils that might be in store. The *Lee's* seamen brought the schooner into the eye of the wind, canvas shaking and slatting. And then, the great booms swung, her sails filled out and she swung into the wake of the slower brigantine.

As she overhauled the stranger, the *Lee* revealed her true colors. At Captain Manley's order, the Dutch flag came fluttering down from the masthead and the Pine Tree Flag went up to take its place.

"Down gunports." Nat sprang to unlash the port and let it swing down on its hinges. As he did so he caught a glimpse of the blocked letters on the brigantine's stern: *Nancy, Liverpool.*

By now the schooner, her gun muzzles snouting out, was almost alongside the *Nancy.* Would the Britisher strike his colors, Nat wondered? There was no indication of surrender yet. Men were dashing about on the *Nancy's* decks, shouting hoarsely.

Captain Manley shouted, "Number one, fire across her bows."

"Br-ooom!" Flame and blue smoke belched from the forward gun. A ball screamed across the *Nancy's* bow to hit the sea beyond in a geyser of water. Still the *Nancy's* colors remained aloft.

"Boarders ready!" The *Lee* surged closer.

Gripping his cutlass firmly, Nat took a deep breath, then dashed to join the fighting men lining the bulwarks.

"Come on, lad," Israel cried. "Swing out at 'em when we go aboard, the same as we did at those hoodlums in Boston——" Then the exultation faded from his voice and he muttered with a groan, "She's striking——"

Sure enough, the Union Jack was being hauled down.

87

A few moments later the *Nancy* came up into the wind, canvas shaking as she lost steerageway. She had surrendered.

As the two vessels wallowed close together on the sea, Captain Manley ordered the longboat manned. To Banty Spooner, picking his boarding party, he said, "Take young Crane with you, Mr. Spooner. I want him to check the cargo."

Reddy Malone, watching, said, "Reckon the skipper heard about young Crane being a Harvard feller and is planning to use him as a clerk."

Israel Boone glared disgustedly as the longboat sheered off and headed for the *Nancy*. "Here I was," he muttered, "all primed for a fight and look what happens."

By nightfall the brigantine's officers and men were aboard the *Lee* as prisoners. A prize crew, commanded by Lieutenant Ogilvy, was aboard the *Nancy* and making ready to sail her to the Massachusetts port of Plymouth.

"We'll be heading for Plymouth too," Joe Patch said as the starboard watch, off duty, sprawled out in the forecastle. "We'll follow along to keep an eye on the *Nancy*."

Reddy Malone was speculating on what the *Nancy's* holds would contain. "Reckon there'll be clothes and blankets which were supposed to keep the lobsterbacks in Boston warm."

"And torches," another seaman said acidly. "The Redcoats need lots of torches so's they can burn up our towns."

"She'll be carrying plenty of salt mutton," Israel commented. "Them Redcoats dote on mutton. Anyway, whatever she's got in her, it'll all be right useful———" He paused as Calvin Crane came down through the scuttle. "Here's the lad who can tell us. What about the *Nancy's* cargo, Calvin? We get anything worthwhile?"

Calvin Crane smiled and nodded. "Captain Manley is more than pleased. I checked off more than two thousand muskets———"

"That's a real haul." Reddy exclaimed.

"And fifty barrels of powder," Calvin went on, "thirty-one tons of musket shot, three thousand round shot, and other things like slow matches, wads, and powder horns. Why, the *Nancy* is a floating arsenal. She's laden with ordnance, too, including several cannon."

"Cannon?" Israel repeated. "Any big ones?"

"I'm not too familiar with such things," Calvin answered, "But one of them was described as a thirteen-inch brass mortar. The captain was most interested in that one."

"He would be," Israel said. "A mortar's a stubby-barreled cannon that can throw a lot of metal. Shoots high, sort of like tossing a rock over a fence." He grinned widely. "I reckon General Washington will just about jump out of his boots when he hears we captured all that ordnance. A few more prizes like the *Nancy* and he'll be making it plenty hot for those lobsterbacks squatting in Boston Town."

CHAPTER NINE

A Message from Jeremy

ON A WARM August afternoon Abigail Harkins stepped outside her kitchen door. Methuselah, the orange cat, was curled on the porch rail where he could take advantage of what little cooling breeze blew in over Boston Town. The cat's ears twitched at the sound of creaking wheels and thumping hoofs. Over the sound of wagon noises Abigail heard the driver whistling.

" 'Yankee Doodle—' " she murmured, her foot tapping in rhythm. "What a crazy name for a song, Methuselah." She reached down and stroked the cat, shaking her head. Crazy name or not, there was no denying that "Yankee Doodle" was a sprightly tune and everybody in Boston was singing it these days.

Some of the neighbors said that some Englishman had written the song to make fun of what they called the "dirty-shirt rebels," and perhaps that was true. Anyway, the patriots had taken it for their own, changing the words to suit themselves. They sang it when they drove the Redcoats and Tories out of Boston last April, after General Washington's guns had magically appeared on Dorchester Heights.

A faraway look came into her eyes when she thought about the patriot's victory in the spring. If it hadn't been for those cannon and ammunition captured at sea by Nat and his mates, things might have been very different.

Thinking of Nat, she smiled happily. He had written to her regularly and, thanks to Caleb Wickerby's couriers, his letters had slipped through the British lines. Of course, there had been delays and times when she had worried herself sick. Things were better, now that Boston was free of the British. Mail was arriving promptly. The letter which Nat had posted from Newburyport last week had come that very morning.

"He's on his way home, Methuselah," she murmured. "He might even be here today and perhaps he'll stay." New England shipyards were beginning to hum. Congress had ordered thirteen frigates built and, according to the Boston *Gazette*, some seventy-four-gun warships were being planned. New privateers would be launched, also, and ships for the State navies. Never would there be a better opportunity for Nat to get started in the shipbuilding trade.

She went back into the house, humming softly. In a few moments she was singing:

> " '*And there was General Washington*
> *Upon a slapping stallion*
> *A-giving orders to his men*
> *I guess there were a million.*
> *Yankee Doodle, keep it up*——' "

Her voice trailed off to silence. Nat was coming home but Jeremy wasn't. Poor Jeremy, ill and suffering in the dank hold of a prison ship in Halifax. Still, she consoled herself, at least he is alive. The message brought by that tattered seaman was proof of that.

She heard footsteps outside. One of the neighbors, probably, coming to borrow flour or sugar. She was about to open the back door when it was flung open and a slender figure with a sea bag on his shoulder strode in, grinning.

"Nat!" she exclaimed happily. "I do declare, Nat Harkins." She ran to him, arms outstretched. When she stepped back she shook her head. "You've grown a few inches, Nat, but you're skinnier than a shadow at sundown. What sort of victuals do they give you on ships, anyway?"

"Mostly salt meat and hard biscuits," Nat said as he put down his sea bag. "Never any apple pie or johnny-cake——"

"You'll have those. It just happens that I've an apple pie in the pantry——" She began bustling about, putting dishes on the table.

The orange cat had followed Nat into the house. When he sat down, the cat leaped into his lap. Stroking Methuselah's fur reminded Nat of Isaiah Nixon and he asked his aunt about the old instrument-maker.

"He's at Concord," Aunt Abigail said. "It wasn't safe for him with all those hoodlums during the British occupation. He ought to be back in his shop in another few weeks."

"And then you'll lose Methuselah, I suppose."

She nodded. "I'll hate to see him go. I haven't seen hide nor hair of a mouse since I've had him. He's good company too."

Nat put the cat down and reached for his sea bag. Untying the rope which secured it, he reached in and brought out a large ham and a round of cheese. "I got these for you from a farm on my way from Newburyport."

"But Nat, you shouldn't have spent so much money."

"I can afford it," Nat said with a note of pride in his voice. "I received my army pay when my enlistment was up. Besides, I've some prize money coming if the courts ever get around to awarding it. Didn't you get my letter telling you not to sell your silver?"

"I didn't sell it," Aunt Abigail said crisply. "I had no call to. A body can always manage. I'm not too proud and I'm right handy with a needle and spinning wheel, if I do say so. I'll manage even better now that the British have gone away from Boston."

"You needn't worry, Aunty," Nat said confidently. "I'll provide for you."

"Does that mean," she asked hopefully, "that you're not going back to sea?"

Nat shook his head. "No, I'll be sailing again. I was hoping to sail with Captain Manley. He is to command one of the new frigates—the *Hancock*. She's named for the President of Congress. Oh, she's a fine vessel. I saw her in Newburyport before I left there. I even talked to Mr. Jonathan Greenleaf, the builder. He's a partner with the Cross Brothers——"

While Nat talked enthusiastically about the frigate *Hancock*, Aunt Abigail brought the pie and cold beans from the pantry and set them on the table.

"She's a wonderful ship-rigged vessel," he went on,

"and nearly a hundred and forty feet long. Of course that's small compared to some of the British men-of-war. Their big seventy-four-gun ships of the line are like floating forts. But the *Hancock* is built for speed. You can tell that from her sheer. I think she'll be the fastest frigate on the seas."

"And you can hardly wait, I reckon, to get aboard of her?"

"I wish I could sail in the *Hancock* with Captain Manley, but it will be months before she's ready. She has to be outfitted and things are hard to get in the colonies these days. Mr. Greenleaf doesn't think she'll sail until next year."

Aunt Abigail brightened. "Then, Nat, don't you think it would be best if you stayed here to learn the shipbuilders' trade? Why, you could be a shipwright's apprentice right here in Boston."

"No, Aunty," Nat said. "With the colonies fighting for independence I must do my share."

"But you would be doing your share. Somebody has to build the ships."

"Boys younger than I and men too old to fight can do that. The rest of us will have to do the fighting." Nat finished his pie and reached for another wedge. "I expect I'll be sailing soon with Israel Boone and Banty Spooner."

Nat told her that Israel and Banty had heard of a fine, fast craft in Portsmouth. They hoped to bring it to Boston soon where the vessel would be outfitted as a privateer.

"A privateer!" she exclaimed. "But, Nat, you can't sail in a privateer. Why, if you are captured you'll be treated as if you were a pirate. You—you might even be hanged."

"Oh, no, Aunty. Most of the colonies have authorized privateers to sail. So has the Continental Congress. We'll carry a commission, called a letter of marque, signed by the President of Congress himself, John Hancock. If we are captured we'll be treated as prisoners of war, not pirates."

She sniffed. "Don't you know, Nat, that England doesn't even recognize the Continental Congress? They'll pay no heed to papers signed by Mr. Hancock. Privateers will be called rebels and pirates if they're caught. But even if they're not hanged, they'll surely be put into one of those terrible prisons." She stopped suddenly. "Nat, I must tell you about Jeremy."

"Jeremy!" Nat sat straight. "Is he——"

"He's alive, but——" She went to a cupboard and returned with a folded slip of paper which she handed to Nat.

"This is Jeremy's handwriting, sure enough," Nat said, glancing at a weak scrawl on the margins of a faded piece of newsprint, "but I can hardly make out the smudged words. There seems to be something about a leg wound and a prison ship."

His aunt nodded. "Jeremy says there that he expects to be sent to England soon. I couldn't have read that part at all if it wasn't for the sailor who brought the message."

"Who was he, Aunty?" Nat asked.

"His name was Jeb Larkin and he was a prisoner with Jeremy. They made plans to escape, but Jeremy's leg was too bad and he was too weak to move. Jeb Larkin

96

told me that the prison ship is a terrible place, alive with rats. All they had to eat was food crawling with maggots and——" Her voice broke.

"Where is Jeb Larkin, Aunty?" Nat asked. "Maybe he'll know some way to help Jeremy. Is he in Boston?"

"No, he sailed off in a privateer, about ten days ago."

Just before dusk, Nat left the Harkins house and headed for the waterfront. As he trudged down the hill along Tremont Street he recalled the wintry night when he and Israel Boone had fled from Boston with the Redcoats at their heels. Over eight months had gone by since they had crossed the back bay and made their way to Cambridge.

His glance ranged out over Boston Harbor. Close in, near the Long Wharf, the bay bristled with the spars of many vessels, as it had last winter. But there was a difference now. Those were Continental craft out there; not grim yellow and black British bulldogs.

Far out to the east, on the rim of the sea, loomed the square upper sails of some vessel hull down on the horizon. That one, Nat reckoned, would be a British warship out of New York. Several frigates and sloops-of-war were patrolling Massachusetts Bay hoping to catch merchant ships or privateersmen. A few had been taken, Nat had heard, although bottling up shipping in an open roadstand like Boston was the same as trying to keep fleas in a birdcage.

Nat descended the slope, hardly recognizing some of the paths he had once known so well. Their appearance had been drastically changed because of the trees and houses which had vanished to provide firewood.

He paused at a corner. Asa Chubb's clapboard house used to be near here and, also, the big apple tree which had provided so many juicy windfalls. He went on and presently saw what was left of the tree—an ax-bitten stump, hewn close to the ground. All that remained of Asa Chubb's house were a few scattered bricks and some broken glass, almost hidden in tall, dry weeds.

Nevertheless it soon became plain to Nat that Boston was fast recovering from the blight of British occupation. Here and there a new fence was being erected.

Horse-drawn carts laden with vegetables and crates of chickens clattered over the cobbles. As he neared the waterfront, Nat's nostrils twitched at the fragrance of molasses and spices. He was thinking that some of the prizes sent in by the privateers must have carried West Indies cargo. Or, perhaps, trade with the Sugar Islands had started again despite the British sea patrols.

Nat saw a half-grown hog, snuffling in some refuse behind a tavern. Gulls circled the wharves and ships, squalling loudly as they quarreled over choice morsels.

Noticing a cluster of sailors reading a placard tacked to a warehouse wall, Nat halted, interested. The sign proclaimed:

> *Prize Money. High Wages. Bonuses for all able-bodied mariners signing in the speedy privateering brig West Wind, 12 guns, now lying at Fletcher's Wharf.*
>
> *Abel Brown & Sons, Owners*

" . . . sail in that rackergaited old tub?" one of the seamen growled. He shook his head so violently that his tarry pigtail swished back and forth. "Not while I got my senses."

"She's a mite cranky," said a hawk-nosed man, pulling at one of his gold earrings. "But she's fast. Remember when we sailed in her to St. Eustatius in the Carribees?"

"She was fast then," was the reply, "but right now her bottom's foul with grass and them Browns are too penny-pinching to careen her."

"Right you are, mate," another man said. "They pinch bellies, too, them Browns. A sea gull would starve to death follerin' a Brown packet." He paused as a drum-and-fife corps approached.

Leading the marchers was a boy carrying a Pine Tree Flag. He had such an air of importance about him that Nat couldn't help but grin. The youngster lifted the banner high as the drums rolled and the corps broke into the lively melody of "Yankee Doodle." Behind the band came some yelling, cavorting urchins and barking dogs.

"They're recruitin' for the Massachusetts State Navy," said a seaman standing next to Nat. "Reckon the *Tyrranicide's* short-handed."

Nat nodded absently. He had seen the *Tyrranicide,* a trim, fast brigantine belonging to the little navy authorized by Massachusetts to try and protect its seaports.

"A man sure has his pick o' ships these days," the seaman said. "Most of the colonies got state navies and they're bellerin' for hands. So's the Continental Navy and the privateers. Which service you hankering for, mate?"

Nat, somewhat flattered at being taken for a real mariner, replied, "I'm signing in a privateer."

The sailor gave his red stocking cap a jerk. "There's plenty like you," he said, "and the prize money's good if a man lives to spend it. But privateerin' ain't for me. Too blamed risky."

Nat went on, noticing the variety of vessels in Boston Harbor. Ships, brigs, schooners, ketches, and snows were either at anchor or tied up to the wharves. Quite a number had splintered spars and patched-up holes in their hulls. Some, Nat reckoned, must be prizes sent in by Continental vessels.

His pace quickened as he neared the Blue Dragon. It would be good to see Caleb Wickerby again. They would have a long talk and—Nat smiled one-sidedly and wondered if Caleb could be persuaded to let Duff sail off on a privateer. Perhaps it hadn't been wise to boast so much about the genial Negro's cooking talents. A dozen times Banty Spooner had said, "Nat, you see to it that Duff sails with us."

Duff would want to go too. Nat was sure of that. Duff was a true patriot. He had known that Jeremy was one of the original Sons of Liberty. He knew about the trouble with Seth Cuffey too.

Thinking of Seth Cuffey, Nat's fists clenched. Where was Cuffey now? Probably he had fled to New York or Canada with the rest of the Tories. But, if by some chance, he was still in Boston, there was an old score to be settled.

Nat squared his shoulders. Months aboard ship had hardened his muscles. He was quite sure that he could deal competently with the porky turncoat.

CHAPTER TEN

The Privateersmen

Turning into Milk Street, Nat headed for the Blue Dragon. He passed by a team of oxen dragging a large dray laden with hewn logs. Glancing at the load with a critical eye, he noted that it consisted of prime yellow pine, which soon would be sawn into timbers for building ships.

Although it was still early, several horses were tethered to the tavern's hitching post. Some carts and carriages were in the yard. The rumble of voices reached Nat's ears as he went in under the swinging signboard on which was painted a fierce blue dragon.

Inside, he glanced about. The place was certainly well patronized. Almost all the tables were occupied by sea captains, businessmen, and officers of the Continental forces. Uniforms, he noticed, were nothing compared to the gaudy, splendid ones worn by the Britishers who had patronized the tavern last winter. Most of the Americans wore homespun coats with collars and cuffs decorated with patches of colored cloth. Rank seemed to be indicated by home-made chevrons of red, green, or blue worn on the shoulders.

At a nearby table was a chubby man in a cherry-colored waistcoat. His hair was neatly clubbed and powdered. Sitting across from him was a tall, bronzed man wearing a flowing green cape. His black pigtail was tied with a yellow ribbon. Huge silver earrings dangled from his pierced ears. A privateer captain, Nat surmised, talking business with a ship owner.

A notice board on the wall near the hearth was filled with placards offering berths in privateers, state cruisers, and naval craft. Examining it were a few swarthy sailors and some buckskin-clad hunters and farmers.

A familiar voice hailed, "Nat! Nat Harkins!" Caleb Wickerby, his wooden leg clumping on the plank floor, hurried forward. Taking Nat's arm, he said, "Come along back to my cubbyhole, lad, where we can talk."

As they went through the pantry, Duff, the cook, exclaimed, "Glory be! If'n it ain't Nat Harkins—browner'n cinnamon and looking like a real sailorman." Duff's face seemed to split in half with a white-toothed grin. "You coming to work here again, Nat? No more dandified Redcoat macaronis 'round to spill chowder on. No more Seth Cuffey either."

"Seth's gone?" Nat felt a twinge of disappointment. "What happened to him, Duff?"

"Nobody knows for sho', Nat. He just done disappeared."

Caleb Wickerby said, "Cuffey disappeared right after the British hauled out of Boston. Some say he signed in a Beverly letter o' marque called the *Alert*. She put in here some time back, looking for a crew."

"It's hard to believe he'd sign in a privateer——"

"Oh, I dunno, Nat." Caleb Wickerby shrugged. "He wouldn't do it out of patriotism, of course. But prize money might be what he's after. Besides, things would've been mighty warm for him here with the Redcoats and Tories gone."

"Wherever Cuffey is," Duff said, "he'll make trouble for sure. That I knows."

The tavern-keeper nodded. "Better get back to your post, Duff, before the crowd out there start chawing on the furniture. You can talk to Nat later."

"Yes, sir. Don't you-all go 'way, Nat."

Caleb Wickerby led Nat to a small room under the staircase and closed the door. "Set down, lad," he said, hooking his cane on a nail in the wall. "Tell me how everything's been going with you. Thought about you considerable. Wished you were here in July when we got word that Congress declared independence. This here town went wild."

"We were at sea then," Nat said. "We didn't hear about that until we reached port——" He paused, remembering how the crew had been called aft, where Captain Manley had announced that the Congress of the thirteen United Colonies, in meeting at Philadelphia, had adopted unanimously the Declaration of American Independence.

"The captain read the Declaration to us," Nat continued. "I can't remember the exact words, but I'll never forget that part about men being created equal and having a natural right to liberty and the pursuit of happiness."

"And also, Nat, that goverments are for the sole purpose of securing the welfare of the people, and not destroying their liberty." The tavern-keeper nodded gravely. "Another thing—that Declaration gave the world all the facts about the unjust treatment these colonies have been getting from King George and Parliament. It shows we don't believe in changing governments unless folks are being oppressed by a tyrant. Then it's not only our right, it's our duty to alter things."

Caleb Wickerby leaned forward, "It's a great document, lad. I heard it read at Faneuil Hall. I got all stirred up inside just like everybody else did. You should have heard the cheering. It was even louder than the bells that were ringing and the cannon booming from Fort Hill and Dorchester Heights. Everybody was hollering so loud I don't doubt but what King George himself heard us clear across the sea."

Nat took a deep breath. "Captain Manley," he said slowly, "after he read the Declaration of Independence, told us that declaring for freedom and getting it were very different. He thought we would have a long, hard fight."

"He's right about that, Nat. And speaking of fighting, I've been hearing some fine reports about Captain Manley and the *Lee*. Folks are saying that if it hadn't been for the prizes you fellers been taking, the Redcoats might still be roosting here in Boston."

"We took some prizes, but so did some of the other

vessels in General Washington's navy. State cruisers like the *Tyrannicide* made captures too."

"True enough. But you grabbed those cannon and ammunition just when General Washington needed 'em. Captain Manley's a real hero to people here in Boston and so's anybody what sailed under him. You going off with him again, Nat?"

Nat explained about the delay in outfitting the frigate *Hancock* and his decision to go privateering.

"Privateering! Now you're talking sense. What vessel you signing in?"

"I'm waiting for Banty Spooner and Israel to return from Portsmouth. They should be here any day now with a fast craft they heard about. She'll outfit and sign a crew here in Boston."

"That Banty is a ding-clicker when it comes to sea fighting, just like Israel is." Caleb Wickerby sighed. "I'd give this tavern and everything in it if I could sail with you fellers. But with this peg leg of mine, I calc'late I'll have to squat right here and be an armchair privateer."

Caleb reached for his cane and pointed to a map tacked to the wall. "I had that map made special, Nat, so I could keep an eye on how things are going. I've got charts of European waters and the Sugar Islands too. Nothing like a good chart to make things clear."

Nat nodded agreement. The northern section of the map was dotted with different-colored tacks which marked the routes of the two colonial armies under Generals Arnold and Montgomery.

"Too bad those two armies got driven back," said the tavern-keeper. "If General Montgomery hadn't got killed, they might have taken Quebec and Canada. But look here, Nat." He pointed again with his cane. "This here's Charleston in North Carolina, down South. That's where the British reckoned to smash the rebels. But two generals—Cornwallis and Clinton—with two fleets of transports loaded with Redcoats and a lot of warships couldn't do the job. Those Georgia and Carolina patriots drove 'em off."

The cane moved northward to New York. "Here's where the Redcoats are now, the whole kit-and-caboodle of 'em. General Howe and his army, and his brother Admiral Howe with hundreds of men-o'-war. Over thirty-five thousand men they've got, not counting the navy. And that's not all. According to Eph Summers, Lord Howe has more'n twelve thousand Hessians in his army now."

"Hessians! Then it's true? The talk I've heard about England sending paid soldiers from a German province. I could hardly believe it."

"No doubt about it, Nat. The royal tyrant is bound and determined to see us knuckle under like proper slaves even if he has to bankrupt the royal treasury by hiring foreigners to shoot us down."

Nat's fists clenched. "How can General Washington hold out against such a force?"

"Reckon he'll have to retreat," Caleb Wickerby said gravely. "His army's got too much smallpox and not enough guns. But he'll make his stand, mark my words. He'll lick the Redcoats soon as the privateers get him more guns and powder——"

He broke off as the door was flung open and Banty Spooner came in, followed by Israel Boone.

"Caleb, you fat crow bait," Banty cackled. "So you been hiding Nat out on us. We've been looking all over Boston for him." He gave Nat a sharp look. "What about Duff, lad?"

Nat began." I—I didn't get a chance to———"

"What about Duff," Caleb Wickerby said. Then he chuckled. "I might've known. Always thinking about victuals, ain't you, Banty? Well, I'll have Duff bring along something."

"Not too much," Banty said. "Just a slab or two off'n that roast you got on the spit, a pot of beans, and some corn bread. Maybe some codfish along with a bowl of chowder. That's all. Sort of off'n my feed today."

"A good thing for me you are," Caleb said drily. He rose, hobbled to the door, and shouted to Duff, then: "Did you fellers get that craft Nat's been telling me about?"

"We got her, Caleb," Israel rumbled. "She's tied up over at Griffith's Wharf. We'll be shoving off for the Indies soon as she's outfitted and we get a crew."

"When can I see her," Nat asked eagerly. "I———"

"After I've et," Banty Spooner said. "I've got to have some strength."

Israel eased into a chair. "Nat, your eyes will pop when you see the *Dauntless*. She's the sweetest little spandy-dandy brig that ever was outfitted to twist the royal lion's tail."

"You got your officers lined up?" Caleb asked.

"We got our skipper," Israel replied. "Joshua Beeler of Portsmouth——"

"Josh Beeler!" Caleb exclaimed. "Why there's not an owner in New England who hasn't tried to get Cap'n Josh to sail with him. How'd you get him?"

Banty chuckled. "We let him buy a part interest in the *Dauntless.*"

"Banty will be first mate," Israel said. "I'll sail second and Reddy Malone will be third. A young feller named Crane who was in the *Lee* with us is going to be our doctor. He ain't a full-fledged sawbones but with doctors scarcer'n fish feathers, he's better than none. Nat here will be the skipper's clerk——"

"Clerk!" Nat protested. "But I expected——"

"More action than a clerk gets, I calc'late," Banty interrupted. "Don't fret, Nat. All hands will be on deck when we engage any Britishers. You'll see plenty of action." He paused as Duff entered with a large tray. Then, turning to Caleb Wickerby he said, "Come to think of it, Caleb, we ain't got a cook yet, and since I got such a sensitive gullet, we need a good one."

"Yes, sir," Duff said, eyes gleaming. "You ought to have somebody like me. If'n I do say so myself I sure can cook and——" He paused, realizing that Caleb was frowning at him.

"You're as good as signed in the *Dauntless,* Duff," Israel said heartily. "We——"

"Now see here," the tavern-keeper said. "I need Duff right here. He——"

"You need him!" Banty Spooner flared. "Where's your patriotism anyway, in your purse? Since you can't go privateering yourself, the least you can do is let Duff go if he wants. And he does." He looked at the cook. "Don't you, Duff?"

"I sure do, only . . ." Duff looked at Caleb uncertainly. "I belong to Mr. Wickerby and I does like he says."

Caleb groaned. "I suppose I do own Duff since I bought him when he was up for sale. But I never did hold with slavery and I never will. So Duff's as free as anybody here. He can sail with you if he wants——"

"Glory be!" Duff did a little jig. With a flashing grin he promised, "Never will you privateerin' fellers have such fine cookin' as you'll get on that *Dauntless.* Yes, sir."

CHAPTER ELEVEN

The *Dauntless,* Privateer

NAT WAS IN THE *Dauntless'* hold, checking off the endless stream of sea stores coming aboard the privateer; ropes, shackles, chains, and canvas; tar, paint, and caulking materials.

Reddy Malone, the privateer's third officer, came striding aft. "Hurry up with those crates," he barked at two huge Negroes who were handling the cargo. "On the double or I'll bash those heads of your together."

The Negroes, members of the crew, grinned widely. Either Ginger or Absalom could have lifted Reddy by the scruff of the neck with one hand and dropped him overboard. They seemed to understand, however, that the new third mate was full of importance with his new authority.

"You got all these items checked off, Nat?" Reddy looked over Nat's shoulder.

"Yes, sir."

"Let's see that list." Reddy snatched the paper. "H'm." He frowned importantly. "We got just about enough to arm a whale boat. Not nearly enough pistols, cutlasses, and boardin' pikes. Mighty shy of sponges, ladles, and wads." He handed the list back. "Watch it, Nat. I wouldn't put it past some of these thieving Boston merchants to short us." He went forward.

Nat wiped his perspiring face with his bandanna. Readying a privateer for sea, he mused, was a gigantic undertaking. The articles coming aboard must number into the thousands. Besides the arms and ammunition and sea stores, provisions had to be accounted for and checked off; casks of salt meat, flour, potatoes, and even livestock. Nat could hear the grunts and cacklings of the small pigs and chickens stowed aft.

Duff was always on hand when the provisions came aboard. He wanted to make sure that everything was properly stowed. Also, he was mighty particular about quality. Only that morning he had said to Nat, "You send that bar'l of flour back ashore. It's full of weevils. I ain't taking those sacks of rotten potatoes either. You privateermen what's fighting bulldogs has got to have good eatables."

Would the *Dauntless* ever be ready for sea, Nat wondered as he began checking a stack of boxes bearing curious labels. He blinked as he glanced at the list: arabic, sal nitre, tincture myrrha, hartshorn, scammony. Then he noticed the consignor's name: Higgins & Cathcart, Apothecaries, and nodded to himself. Those were medical stores, and they didn't belong in the hold.

"Ahoy, mate!" Calvin Crane came down the companionway. He saw the supplies. "So this is where my stores got to. I've been searching high and low for them."

"Ginger and Absalom were bringing them down. I guess they didn't know——"

"Yes, suh," Absalom said. "Ginger's been tossin' 'em down to me and——"

"Tossing them!" Calvin exclaimed. "Jumping Jupiter, Absalom. Don't you know what would happen if you ever dropped some of this basilicum or epispastic?" He paused dramatically. "Well, I'll tell you. The whole ship would have gone up in smoke!"

The two sailors looked at each other. Ginger said, "I don't read so good. What ones are 'silicum and 'pastic?"

Calvin Crane gestured widely. "All those boxes are dangerous. When you take them up to my cubbyhole be sure to handle them carefully, understand?"

"Yes, suh." Cautiously they each took a box and went off on tiptoe.

When they were out of earshot Nat asked, "Would some of those medicines really explode, Calvin?"

"No," Calvin grinned. "I just wanted to make sure that my stores wouldn't be damaged. Some of those boxes contain bottles and vials which aren't easily obtained. We can't afford any breakage." He eased down on a keg and leaned back against the bulkhead. "Nat, I've overheard some scuttlebutt gossip. It's said that we may be sailing before dawn tomorrow."

"But that's impossible, Calvin," Nat exclaimed. "We're still short of sidearms and powder. Actually, we've no cannon except those old four-pounders that nobody else wants."

"I think that Captain Beeler may be counting on getting his guns and powder elsewhere than in Boston.

Haven't you noticed those two Frenchmen who have been spending considerable time aboard?"

Nat nodded. "I've seen them. They were in the captain's cabin this morning."

"Monsieur Dupré and Monsieur Larue. Those dapper gentlemen, Nat, might well represent French business interests hoping to sell munitions to the colonies."

"But how can they?" Nat asked. "Hasn't France some kind of a treaty with England which prohibits the shipment of arms to us?"

"You mean the Treaty of Paris which was signed after the French and Indian War." Calvin Crane smiled crookedly. "The French don't think much of that treaty. They lost heavily by it. In fact, it cost them Canada for one thing."

"And you think that France, to get back at England, might help the colonies to get their independence?"

"I'm sure of it, Nat," Calvin said. "Certain men in our Continental Congress know this. That's why they've sent Silas Deane to Paris. He will be known as the American Commissioner there, and there has been talk of sending Benjamin Franklin also. Their real work will be to arrange French aid."

A voice bellowed down the companionway. "Calvin Crane. Dr. Calvin Crane and Nat Harkins wanted in the cabin on the double!"

Nat and Calvin clambered up the ladder and made their way aft to the officers' quarters. They had hardly reached the captain's cabin when the two Frenchmen emerged. Nat heard Monsieur Dupré saying:

"Do not forget, Captaine Beelaire, that when you have

113

delivery of the—the cargo—you mus' have ready the cash money."

"Cash it'll be, Monsoor," came the captain's deep, gravelly voice. "Cash on the barrelhead."

"*Adieu* then, and *bon voyage*." The Frenchmen left.

The captain, seeing Nat and Calvin, beckoned. "Come in, you two," he growled.

Captain Beeler sat at the head of the table which was strewn with papers. He was a blocky man with wide shoulders. His icy blue eyes peered out from a face which seemed carved from rock.

Flanking him at the table were Banty Spooner and Israel Boone. Next to them sat Reddy Malone and the sailing master, Asa Widgeon.

"Set down, lads," said the captain gruffly. "We've a passel of things to do if we expect to slip out of Boston tonight."

Tonight! Nat's eyes widened. Apparently they were sailing within hours.

"Captain Beeler," said Sailing Master Widgeon in a squeaky voice. "I think we are acting unwisely in tryin' to sail tonight. We're not ready yet."

"Now look here, Asa." Captain Beeler pounded on the table with a hamlike fist. "We just arranged to buy some heavy cannon and munitions from them two Frenchies— long eighteens and sixes that'll make it plenty hot for British commerce. But those guns are at Cap François in Saint-Domingue. So we've got to go there to get 'em."

"But it's dangerous," Asa Widgeon protested, "sailing in these waters practically unarmed. The British patrol ships——"

"We're not worried about them, Asa." Israel Boone

114

broke in. "We'll steer clear of them two bulldogs hanging off Boston. There's no moon tonight."

"But the picaroons," Asa Widgeon squeaked. "The waters around the Sugar Islands are alive with them."

"Sure enough, Asa," Banty Spooner said. "They're thicker'n flies around a broached molasses barrel, especially in the Windward and Caicos Passages. But I reckon our four-pounders ought to take care of 'em."

"Right you are," Captain Beeler agreed. "Anybody who's a-feared of a few pirates better stay home and knit socks." He glanced down the table toward Nat. "Lad, I'm having the crew summoned aft. I want you to check off their names on the crew list and make notes on their nearest kin in case any of 'em get killed." To Calvin Crane he said, "And you, Doctor, go over every last man from stem to stern. Any of 'em who look like they might have the pox or something else will have to be sent ashore."

"But, Cap'n," said Reddy Malone. "We can't turn a man down just because he might have the sniffles or look a mite peaked. We're short-handed as it is. We——"

Captain Beeler's fist thumped the table again. "Confound it, sometimes I wonder if you have any sense, Mr. Malone. Don't you know that one man with a catching ailment can put the whole crew on their backs, or worse? We've got enough to do without fighting disease. Besides, we'll likely be able to sign on some foreigners at Cap François."

He handed Nat the crew list and snapped to Israel Boone. "All right, Mr. Boone. Tell the bos'n to pipe all hands aft."

CHAPTER TWELVE

The Picaroons

BLOWN BY A gentle breeze, the *Dauntless* was sailing through the Bahama Channel toward the island called Saint-Domingue. Captain Beeler had decided to run down past Florida and then shape a southeasterly course north of Cuba to reach Cap François.

For one thing, the pirates weren't so plentiful in these waters. Mostly they infested the Caicos Islands to the east where the pickings were better. Besides, the Bahama Channel enabled the *Dauntless* to stay close to the coast which offered havens in the event of a chase by a British bulldog.

Nat Harkins was in the cabin. Little rivulets of sweat trickled down his face and neck as he worked on a list of sea stores and provisions. These items would be procured in Cap François, if possible.

Finishing the list, Nat rose and handed it to Captain Beeler who, with Sailing Master Widgeon, was poring over a chart of the West Indies. Nat was hoping that the captain wouldn't give him any more clerical work for a spell. Some fresh air was what he needed. Surely it would be cooler on deck.

As he gave the captain the list, Nat couldn't help but glance curiously at the chart. Islands! Nothing but islands and reefs. Hundreds of them dotted the waters off Florida and clear down to the Carribean Sea.

Noticing Nat's interest, the captain grunted, then: "Like to know where we are, lad?" He pointed. "Right here, off the north coast of Cuba."

Cuba, Nat saw, was one of the two truly large islands in the West Indies. The other was Saint-Domingue. These two large islands, sprawling generally east and west, faced each other across the Windward Passage, which led down into the Carribean Sea.

Saint-Domingue reminded Nat of a gigantic crab whose claws were outstretched to engulf a small prey which was called Gonave Island. Cuba, on the west side of the Windward Passage, resembled a huge shovel-nosed shark about to dispute the crab's right to the morsel.

To the north lay a bewildering cloud of islets, reefs, and shoals of all sizes and shapes. These were the Bahamas. To the south, and almost alone in the vastness of the Carribean Sea, was the fairly large island of Jamaica, England's main stronghold and supply base in the West Indies.

"Look here, Captain," Asa Widgeon frowned at the chart. "I'm a mite worried about our crossing that Windward Passage."

The captain sighed. "You worry about everything, Asa," he said. "Why not let me do the fretting for a change?"

"But, Captain, the Windward Passage is the main British route to Jamaica from England. Bulldogs will be on patrol there——"

"Don't you suppose I know that?" was the irritated reply. "We'll cross the Windward Passage at night. Nothing else we could do anyway."

Nat had been trying to find New Providence. That was another British island in the Bahamas which had been raided early in the year by the Continental Navy under Commodore Esek Hopkins. However, the captain grunted again and, in a tone of dismissal, said, "You can go on deck if you want, Nat. I'll have no more work for you until tonight."

"Yes sir," Nat said gratefully. He went forward and up a companionway to the deck where a blazing sun was blistering the deck and causing the tar to ooze out from between the seams. Although it seemed no cooler topside than below, he no longer felt so miserably uncomfortable. The light breeze was partially responsible, but mostly it was because of the beauty of the southern sea.

He gazed raptly out at the endless green swells. He watched the flying fish that looked like slivers of gleaming silver as they skittered for incredible distances over the surface. Near the ship a huge turtle floated serenely with a long-legged sea bird perched on his back.

"Peaceful, isn't it, Nat?"

Nat turned to see Calvin Crane lounging in the shade of an awning lashed to one side of the galley.

"It is," Nat agreed. When the *Dauntless* sailed from Boston she seemed to have left the war behind. Some friendly privateers and a Rhode Island state cruiser had been spoken. Once the lookouts had sighted the topsails of a big three-master which might have been a bulldog, but the next morning she had vanished. Not a pirate had been seen.

"Nat," Calvin said sharply, "come over here in the shade or I'll be treating you for sunstroke."

Nat sprawled down beside the young doctor and grinned. "About time you did some work, Calvin. The whole crew envies you."

"They don't know how lucky they are that this is a healthy ship," was the reply. "I imagine, though, I'll have my work cut out before this cruise is over."

Duff, the cook, emerged from the galley with a wooden slops pail, which he emptied over the side to windward. "Sure is splendiferous weather," he commented, "except I don't reckon you snowbirds appreciate it." He glanced over the bow. "Looks like a squall a-coming to cool us off pretty quick."

Nat rose to see a long dark cloud on the rim of the sea ahead. It grew even as he watched, spreading and rising like the wings of a mammoth bat. All along its base was a ribbon of white where the sea was being roiled by the wind.

The boatswain's whistle peeped and the crew began swarming aloft to get canvas off the brig.

"Crickety," Duff muttered, "she's a-coming fast. I better tie down my pots." He darted into the galley.

A stillness came over the sea. The air was sticky and oppressive. The sounds of gear being secured, voices, footsteps came loud and clear.

A sword of yellow light stabbed down through the murk ahead. Seconds later came the clap and resounding boom of thunder. The cloud mass rose higher, dark fingers reaching toward the white disk of the sun.

Suddenly a fierce gust of wind ruffled the sea close by and the brig heeled, canvas slatting, gear creaking. A long green swell, like a moving mountain, surged toward the vessel.

Nat braced himself as the bows lifted and the *Dauntless* reeled and pitched. Lightning slashed down again followed by deafening thunder. The first drops of rain pattered on the awning and dotted the deck. The sun paled and then was swallowed by the storm cloud and an eerie twilight came over the sea.

The squall broke in a raging fury. Timbers creaking, gear pounding, the brig rolled wildly in the boiling sea. Weird, screeching wails came from the rigging, which vibrated in the wind like gigantic violin strings. The canvas awning, ripped off by the gale, blew skyward in shreds.

The rain came in a sudden drenching torrent, gurgling and bubbling down through the scuppers. Within seconds Nat was as wet as though he had fallen overboard. He followed Calvin, clawing his way toward the shelter of the galley.

Inside, Calvin said shakily, "If this lasts much longer we'll be at the bottom."

Duff, trying to still his clattering pots, laughed. "This ain't nuthing," he said. "You should see some of the hurricanes here in the Indies. I saw one once that blew down every house in Porto Plata and killed hundreds of folks.

This here is only a measly squall. It's blowing out already."

The cook proved to be right. The sky was growing lighter and soon the wind began to subside. Before long the sun was shining brightly again and the only evidence of the squall was a roily sea and clouds of steam rising from the swiftly drying decks.

In the morning the *Dauntless* was becalmed. She lay almost motionless on the glassy sea about two miles off a group of small islands and reefs which flanked the high bluffs of the Cuban mainland.

Nat was on deck with Calvin Crane when Israel Boone came striding forward, a spyglass under his arm. Pausing, the big mariner lifted the glass and aimed it at the nearest island.

"I reckon that'll be Cayo Cruz, lads," he said. "Most of these cayos—that's what the Spanishers call small islands—are deserted, except for a few bands of picaroons. Let's hope there's none around here. With us becalmed——" He handed the glass to Nat. "Here, have a look."

Nat leveled the spyglass and saw a shoreline which was mostly rocky. A few clusters of palms grew here and there and some low bushes. Flocks of sea birds fluttered over the island and nearby reefs.

Calvin took the glass. "Bleak-looking country this north coast of Cuba," he murmured. "I"—he paused, then—"I thought I saw something moving just beyond that clump of palms near the tip of the island."

Israel reached for the telescope and lifted it. "Sure enough," he exclaimed. "A small boat's putting out."

"Pirates?" Nat asked excitedly.

"Could be," said Israel grimly. "Still, I can see only one boat. Picaroons would send out a whole passel of boats and canoes to board a becalmed craft like us."

The boat was in plain sight now, rounding the northern shore of the cayo. Sunlight glinted from dripping oars as the boat headed directly for the brig. As it came closer, Nat saw that it was a whaleboat manned by a crew of seven—a steersman in the sternsheets and six rowers, three to a side.

The *Dauntless'* crew lined the bulwarks and stared curiously as the strange little craft hauled up off the starboard beam.

"Mean-lookin' outfit," muttered a seaman standing next to Nat.

The oarsmen, their dark, naked bodies gleaming, stared at the brig with insolent expressions. Apparently they were natives of mixed blood. Some wore tattered straw hats. Others had colored bandannas wrapped around their heads. Shiny ornaments dangled from their ears.

"They don't seem to be armed at least." Nat said.

A huge figure arose in the stern of the whaleboat and waved an arm. "Ahoy the brig," he shouted with a Spanish accent. "What you want? What you got? You make the trade?"

Even as he spoke, he dropped back into the sternsheets and the oarsmen, dipping their blades again, began pulling closer to the *Dauntless*.

From aft came the rumble of Captain Beeler's voice: "Sheer off."

"But we come aboard to make the trade," the big steerman replied. He ordered his crew to stop rowing and all of them held up baskets of limes and some pink feathery objects. "Fine limes. Bird of Paradise skin. We come aboard and show you——"

"No, you don't," Captain Beeler roared. "Try to come aboard my ship and you'll feel cold steel. Off with ye now."

The whaleboat pulled off and then began a slow, wide circle of the brig.

Duff shook his head. "I sure don't trust them folks. No, sir. They don't look like no traders I ever saw in the Indies."

"You're right, Duff," said Israel as the whaleboat headed back toward the island. "They look more like slaves who escaped from the sugar plantations and turned pirate. I'll feel a lot better when we get a breeze so's we can haul out of here."

"But there's only a handful of them," Calvin Crane said. "Surely they couldn't hope to overpower us."

"We saw only them what was in that boat," Israel said. "But there might be hundreds of them and lots more boats lurking in those channels and reefs between the islands and the mainland. I don't like the way they circled around us, either. They might have been a scouting party sent out to look us over."

Captain Beeler, evidently, shared Israel's opinion. Before darkness fell, he ordered pistols and cutlasses issued. The longboat was manned and two anchors were dropped into the sea, one to port, the other to starboard.

"Those are to haul the brig around if any pirates try to board us," Israel explained.

Nat understood. Pirates would approach the brig toward the bow or stern so that the cannon couldn't be aimed at them. With a sheet anchor out, however, the vessel could be hauled around with the capstan and thereby bring her guns to bear on any approaching foe.

Night came swiftly. Twinkling stars began needling through the black velvet of the sky. All hands, except those needed below, were on deck, sprawled on blankets and with their weapons handy. A strict watch had been ordered and dozens of pairs of eyes scanned the sea in all directions.

Nat was stationed in the bow, an important post. He crouched down in the still, sultry night, his eyes constantly sweeping the silver-specked sea. He wondered how he could ever see a hostile craft out there. As for hearing one, that seemed impossible. Those fellows he had seen were expert oarsmen. With muffled oarlocks they could come alongside without anyone being the wiser.

The hours dragged by. At intervals the ships bells clanged out the time. A night bird croaked overhead, and Nat rubbed his eyes, fighting sleepiness.

Hearing footsteps, he turned to see Banty Spooner and Reddy Malone, pale figures in the starlight. They were making the rounds to see that the lookouts were awake.

"Nothing to report, eh, Nat?" Banty clacked. "Well, you watch for any dark hulk moving out there, or any phosphorescence in the sea which wasn't there before."

"This here is a lot of tom-foolishness if you ask me," Reddy Malone muttered. "Those fellers wasn't any more pirates than we are. Why, if I was skipper of this here packet——"

"A good thing you're third mate, Reddy," Banty

interrupted. "If you was skipper likely we'd all have our gizzards slit before morning. These Sugar Island pirates can swarm up a ship's side like ants up a wall. And they don't leave any evidence that'd hang 'em if they ever got caught. Keep your eyes peeled, Nat."

A while later the ship's bells clanged: *Ding Ding*. Two bells. Eleven o'clock.

Nat was startled by a splash and a ribbon of phosphorescence off the bow, but as it disappeared he breathed easier. A big fish probably. Perhaps a shark chasing some smaller fry. A falling star streaked down and vanished. Nat yawned.

Suddenly he stiffened. Was that a silvery streak moving out there? He fixed his gaze on the area. Perhaps it was only star reflections. His eyes blurred and he blinked. Then he saw it again, and knew it for what it was: phosphorescent light, caused by millions of tiny sea creatures when they were disturbed.

His pulse pounded. Something was moving on the sea, something V-shaped. A boat's bow could well be disturbing the sea creatures. He gasped as he saw another moving streak. And another. He leaped to his feet shouting:

"Pirates! Pirates, approaching the bow!"

The warning was echoed aft. The boatswain's whistle shrilled. Feet pounded the deck as harsh orders rang out:

"Hands forward to repel boarders."

"Starb'd anchor heave away."

"Battle stations."

"Larboard gun crews ready."

The first boat, filled with howling pirates, was under

the bows. A grappling hook whizzed past Nat's head and thumped down behind him. The line attached to the hook tautened and Nat slashed away at it with his cutlass. Before he could cut the rope a dark head appeared over the rail as the first pirate tried to board the brig.

Nat struck out desperately and the shadowy figure fell away. More heads appeared and he hacked away at clawing hands. Suddenly the line parted and several pirates, shrieking wildly, dropped into the sea.

More grappling hooks swished over and found a hold. More pirates came clambering up. But Nat was no longer alone now. Banty Spooner and his men surged to the bow, cutlasses flashing as they slashed at heads, hands, and arms.

The pirates kept coming. If they were driven back to starboard, they came swarming up the larboard side.

"At 'em, lads," Banty Spooner yelled. "Keep 'em off. Give 'em steel, you codfish eaters, or we'll all be shark bait by morning."

Someone shouted hoarsely, "They're aboard——"

Now it was hand-to-hand fighting on the brig's deck. Nat heard Israel's deep-throated roaring mingling with the howls of the picaroons. Knives flashed, pistols barked, and then came the roar of the *Dauntless'* cannon.

"More boats coming," Reddy Malone yelled. "A dozen at least."

The cannon thundered again and Nat found himself hoping that the gunners would find their targets. If not . . .

A giant figure was almost upon Nat. He saw a fierce, scarred face looming close. He heard a grunting curse then; "*Mort!* Death!" A steel blade gleamed just as Nat thrust out his cutlass. Steel rang against steel, and a searing stab of pain smote his shoulder. He fell headlong. Voices and sounds grew fainter. Was the battle over, he wondered vaguely? He couldn't think any more. He only knew that everything was strangely quiet, and then there was only blackness.

CHAPTER THIRTEEN

Cap François

NAT WAS ON deck when the *Dauntless* stood into the French colonial port of Cap François. Sudden pain stabbed his left shoulder as he made his way to the bulwarks where some of the crewmen were staring curiously shoreward. Man alive, but that wound hurt sometimes. Still, it might have been worse, he knew. If he hadn't managed to partially parry that big pirate's cutlass with his own, he might have lost his arm.

He was wondering what might have happened to the *Dauntless* if she hadn't been ready for the pirates. The cruise might have ended then and there. According to Reddy Malone, there had been two or three hundred picaroons. The way he talked, you'd think he'd beaten them off single-handed. He had put up a good fight though.

Duff came out of his galley. "Nat," he said, "sure good to see you on deck again. How are you feeling?"

"Sort of weak, Duff." Nat managed to grin. "But I guess I'm lucky I wasn't killed or badly wounded like some were."

Duff nodded. "They's still some poor fellers in sick

bay. A good thing that Doc Crane was aboard. He sewed you up neater'n a sailmaker mending a rip in the canvas." He looked toward the town which was growing rapidly as the brig neared her anchorage. "Sure is pretty, ain't it?"

Cap François was built on the shore of a bright, blue-green bay. From all around the town sun-bleached hills sheered up to join jagged green and purple mountains. Colorful houses dotted the flat land and slopes. They were carelessly scattered as if some giantess, astride one of those crags, had tossed down a handful of vividly colored beads. Near the bay, though, the buildings were in more orderly rows. Those, Nat surmised, were the warehouses and stores that served the ships.

"Cap François appears to be a busy port, Duff," Nat commented as he looked over the shipping in the harbor. Already the brig was slipping past vessels flying the French, Dutch, Spanish, and other foreign flags.

His attention was caught by a Pine Tree emblem drooping from the gaff of a sleek-looking sloop. On her counter were the blocked letters, *Defiance, Gloucester*. Near the *Defiance* lay the brigantine *Dolly* out of Scituate.

Duff gestured. "Over there, Nat." He pointed past the *Dolly*. "Hasn't that brown sloop got the name *Alert* painted on her stern?"

Nat squinted. "Sure enough, Duff. She's the *Alert*, out of Beverly———"

"And that's the privateer what Seth Cuffey is supposed to be in, Nat. Maybe that trouble-maker is still aboard."

Nat's jaw tightened at the mention of Cuffey. By golly, if he weren't so weak from the loss of blood he would look up that fat turncoat and take his measure. Maybe he would do it anyway.

Just ahead loomed a huge warship. Nat and Duff had to tilt their heads back to look up at her. Nat was admiring the gilded carving on her stern when Israel Boone came by and paused.

"She's called *La Furieuse*," Israel said. "A French first-rater. Look at them gunports. Why, she'll mount over a hundred cannon and she'll have more'n a thousand men to man her."

"A thousand!" Duff exclaimed. "Crickety. A man sure would have a time cooking for all those fellers."

"I reckon they've got more'n one cook aboard, Duff," Israel said drily.

Soon the *Dauntless* glided to her anchorage. The anchor rattled down and the crew went about their business of securing the brig for a stay in port. That was when Captain Beeler sent for Nat and asked, "Feel up to going ashore, lad?"

"Yes, sir," Nat replied, eager for a look at the tropical port.

"Good." The captain handed Nat several sealed envelopes for delivery ashore. "Young Doc Crane will go with you. He needs some medical supplies for one thing. And he's learned to speak French at Harvard. You two keep together. There's villains in Cap François who'd bash in your skull just to get your shoes."

With Nat and Calvin aboard, the longboat pushed

through a cluster of canoes and small boats hovering near the boarding ladder. These belonged to the bumboatmen, who were continually crying their wares in broken English mixed with French. Some had fruit for sale—pineapples, bananas, and limes. Others offered caged parrots, baskets, and straw hats. One peddler had his boat filled with large turtles which Duff had been eying with interest.

"Clear the way," the boatswain shouted. The longboat shot past the peddlers and soon pulled up at a coral wharf, where Nat and Calvin scrambled ashore.

"Business first, Nat," Calvin said as they walked off the wharf. "We'll deliver those envelopes, then look for some medicines I need. After that we'll have a look around." Taking the envelopes, he glanced at the addresses. "These firms are both on the same street—Rue Bonne."

Calvin hailed a pair of passing French soldiers and queried them in rapid French.

"*Oui, Oui, M'sieur.*" One of the soldiers replied, gesturing, "Rue Bonne."

"*Merci.*"

They pushed on through a throng of peddlers and children who seemed intent upon blocking their way. Inside of an hour, however, the letters were delivered and Calvin Crane's medical supplies ordered at an apothecary shop.

Cap François, Nat was thinking as they went leisurely along the waterfront, was probably the strangest place in all the world. When he mentioned this to his companion, however, Calvin smiled. "Strange sights, Nat. Strange people, strange smells. Still, these folks might think Boston somewhat strange too."

Boston! Nat sighed. It seemed to him that Boston must be on some other planet. He resolved that the moment he returned to the ship he would write to his aunt and to Caleb Wickerby. The captain had told him that some of the trading vessels in port would be taking mail northward.

How long, he wondered, before he would hear from home? Not for many months probably. According to the scuttlebutt gossip aboard ship, the *Dauntless* would range in mid-Atlantic and then head for European waters. Letters might be expected in France, Spain, or Holland, where they would be held for the privateersmen by Colonial representatives.

A pair of sailors swaggered by—New England privateersmen by the look of them—chewing on sticks of sugar cane they had apparently bought from one of the hundreds of peddlers. A thin Negro woman, with a basket slung over her shoulder, clawed at Nat's arm. "You buy my charm, *mes amis*. You buy charm and nevaire will you die in war."

They were accosted constantly by clamoring natives who insisted upon being their guides. They saw elegantly dressed native women and girls, strolling under colored parasols and pausing at shops displaying bonnets and laces. The scent of their perfume was startling to Nat, who wasn't used to such things. Evidently the men wore perfume, too, since he got an occasional whiff of it from a passing French dandy.

Predominant, though, were the odors of sugar and coffee. Nat knew these scents from the Boston wharves, but here in Cap François, the reek of them was like a fog. These aromas, mingled with the smell of decaying fish, ripe fruit, and perfume made him a little dizzy.

As they paused to let a horse-drawn cart piled high with sacks of coffee go by, Calvin said, "I imagine that Christopher Columbus would be surprised if he could see Cap François today. When he landed on this island, there were only wild Carib Indians to greet him."

"Indians? But I haven't seen anyone who looks like an Indian, Calvin."

"They're a vanished race, Nat. They were wiped out by the Spanish adventurers."

"Spanish adventurers? But Cap François is French."

"Years ago this island belonged to Spain and was called Santo Domingo. Later this part of the island was ceded to France——" Calvin paused as they approached an open area where tables and chairs were set out in the shade of palm trees. "An outdoor café, Nat. Shall we try their coffee?"

Nat agreed eagerly, glad for a rest. His arm and shoulder was bothering him and he felt weak from the stifling heat. The café was well patronized, but they found a vacant table behind some palms where a native girl brought them small cups of black coffee sweetened with molasses. Through the palm fronds they could see that other tables were occupied by soldiers, sailors, and Frenchmen in spic-and-span white suits.

Nat was sipping his coffee when he heard a familiar

voice. "This way, Toby," the voice was saying. "Over here where we can talk quietlike."

Nat sat straighter. There was no mistaking the smooth, oily voice of Seth Cuffey. He caught a flashing glimpse of the turncoat who was leading his burly companion to a table beyond the screen of palms.

"Who is it, Nat?" Calvin asked. "Someone you know——"

"Sh——" Nat put a finger to his lips as the big man with Cuffey growled, "Wish I was back in Boston Town, Seth. This heat's killing me."

Nat gritted his teeth. He knew that voice too. He wouldn't forget the man called Toby who had led the mob of so-called Liberty Boys when they almost beat poor Isaiah Nixon to death.

"I reckon a man can stand a little heat when there's money to be made." Cuffey gave a short laugh. "Those guns and barrels o' powder are aboard the *Alert* right now. Later we'll see that Monsoor Lebrun and get our money."

"I don't trust that Frenchy," Toby muttered. "More'n likely the powder's half sand and those old cannon he sold us will blow apart the first time——"

"Don't be such a bufflehead, Toby," Cuffey interrupted. "You don't expect the monsoor to sell first-grade stuff and make a profit for us as well as for himself, do you?"

"Jumpin' Jupiter, Seth. We're the ones who got to fight the bulldogs in that privateer. I ain't risking my neck with old cannon and——"

"You won't be risking as much as a fingernail, Toby. You and me won't be aboard the *Alert* when she shoves off from here today."

"We won't?"

Seth grunted. "Must be the heat's affecting your mind. Didn't we have it all planned from the start? Didn't we sign in the *Alert* so's we could get here and rake in a fortune?"

"Sure," Toby admitted. "But I still don't like it. Those fellers in the *Alert* are mostly New Englanders like us and——"

"Aw, pipe down, Toby. Just think about those hundreds of privateers that'll be putting in here or at Mole St. Nicholas and other Frenchie ports to buy powder and guns. Why, we'll be rich enough to buy Boston Town 'fore this year is out."

"I—I reckon so," Toby said hesitantly. "If we don't get that money, somebody else will."

Listening, Nat's pulse beat fast. The thing to do, he knew, was to slip away and warn the captain of the *Alert*. There wasn't much time either. The *Alert* had been getting ready to sail when he had last seen her.

"Come on, Calvin," Nat rose. "We've got to get aboard the *Alert*."

They were about to leave when a little boy selling sugar cane poked his head through the palm fronds. "You like nice cane, sars," he piped. "The very finest, the most sweet——"

Nat was about to make a run for it when he heard Cuffey's startled shout: "Somebody's behind those palms,

137

Toby. Let's have a look." He turned to see the turncoat thrusting through the palms followed by the towering hulk of Toby.

"Wal, if it ain't our little Tory friend Nat Harkins o' Boston," Seth grinned one-sidedly. "How long you been lurkin' here, Harkins?"

"Long enough," Nat snapped. "Come on, Calvin. I never did like to be around skunks."

"Oh, no, you don't." Cuffey began edging around the table. "Like as not you'll be heading for the *Alert* with some crazy yarn to tell the skipper. Not that he'd listen to a Tory spy like you, but there's no point taking chances. Jump the tall one, Toby. We'll knock 'em cold and carry 'em out. We'll say they was laid low by the heat. Then we'll lock 'em in Lebrun's warehouse and——"

While he talked, Cuffey's fist lashed out, grazing Nat's jaw. Nat struck back and, hearing Seth's muffled oath, knew he had landed a telling blow. A couple more like that and—he reeled. The pain in his shoulder was almost unbearable. Gritting his teeth, he swung again and Cuffey staggered back, knocking over the table.

The crash brought the proprietor of the café on the run. *"Non! Non!"* he cried. "Someone call *les gendarmes*——"

A crowd began gathering, watching Calvin Crane skillfully evading Toby's bearlike clumsy thrusts. Soon there was a circle of curious onlookers, including some privateersmen. One of the latter shouted, "Is this here a private scuffle or can anybody get in on it?"

"Call *les gendarmes*," squealed the proprietor, dancing about wildly.

An instant later a heavy earthen urn sailed through the air and crashed into Nat's head. He staggered and as he sank to his knees he heard a nasal New England voice, "That ain't fightin' fair, you fat baboon. Come on, mates, let's us even things up some."

"Look here, you fellers," Seth Cuffey cried. "You know me. You know my ship. These here fellers, they're plain no-good. My mate and I run into 'em in Boston Town. They're Tory spies, that's what."

"That's not true," Calvin Crane said hotly. "Captain Beeler of the *Dauntless* can vouch for us. We—"

"Listen to that smooth talk," Seth chortled. "He sure sounds like one of them King-lovers." Encouraged by a murmur of assent, Seth went on. "Come on, you fellers.

Help us lock up these two spies in Lebrun's warehouse."

Nat had managed to struggle to his feet again. Through a kind of red mist he saw the triumphant smile on Cuffey's round face. A wild anger surged through him and he plunged forward, only to stagger again. Toby's fist lashed out.

Nat was aware of a roaring sound in his ears. Over it came a familiar, rumbling voice. He knew that Israel Boone was speaking, but he couldn't follow what was being said. The words were meaningless. So were the noises which followed. It wasn't until he felt himself being carried that words began to make sense.

Israel was saying, "He's coming to, Doc. A lot sooner, I reckon, than them other two will. Never enjoyed anything much more than cracking them two noggins together."

CHAPTER FOURTEEN

The Sea Wolves

IT WAS FLYING-FISH weather in the Atlantic. The sapphire blue of the sea was broken by only a slight ripple. The privateer *Dauntless,* ranging well to the south of Bermuda, was pacing a westbound British convoy whose forest of spars could be seen lifting on the rim of the horizon.

Peering at the distant squadron, Nat Harkins counted twenty sails. There were many more, probably, but since they were huddled so close together he had difficulty making them out.

In the southeast, the early sun glinted on another patch of canvas. That would belong to the Colonial privateer *Carnation.* Off to the west another privateer, the *Yankee,* was sailing smartly. All three were hovering near the convoy, hoping for stragglers. Like wolves, Nat was thinking. Cunning wolves skirting the edge of a flock of sheep, always with one eye on the shepherd.

Nat fixed his gaze on the shepherd—a large vessel, ship-rigged. She would be a frigate, probably, or at least a sloop-of-war. Given the chance, her heavy guns could send all three privateers to the bottom without half trying.

"When it comes to taking prizes out of a big convoy like that one, Nat," Israel Boone had said, "several privateers are better than one. If the shepherd starts after one of us, the others can rush in and make captures."

"Looks as if the captain of that ship knows that," Nat said, squinting at the squadron. "He's staying so close to the convoy that we can't even get close without coming within range of his cannon."

"Just be patient, lad. Fair weather won't hold much longer. The sea's quiet now, and those merchant ships can sail close together. Let a blow come and they'll scatter. Then we'll start grabbing off the strays."

Nat was beginning to think that this particular convoy would reach Jamaica intact. The *Dauntless* was barely moving across the flat expanse of sea.

He looked aft where the gun crews were being trained to handle the new guns which had been put aboard the privateer at Cap François. The cannon were monsters compared to the little four-pounder he had learned to man. In addition to the eighteen-pounders, several six-pounders had been acquired, and a number of new brass swivels. Mounted on the bulwarks or in the tops, the little swivels could be aimed in any direction to spray the decks of a nearby enemy with a hail of lead pellets.

The crew had been enlarged too. The *Dauntless* had sailed from Boston with about sixty men, ordinarily a large crew for a brig under three hundred tons' burden, but still not nearly enough for a privateer. In Cap François a number of French creoles and free Negroes anxious to fight for the American cause had been signed on. Now the *Dauntless* carried a hundred men.

"And we'll need every man Jack of 'em too," Israel said. "For fighting and to sail our prizes back to port. By the time we reach European waters—if we have any luck at all—we'll be down to a skeleton crew."

As he watched Israel instructing the men in gunnery, Nat felt a sudden surge of anger against Seth Cuffey. Had it not been for that rascally turncoat Nat might be learning to man one of the big eighteen-pounders right now. But his wound had opened up during the scuffle in Cap François. According to Calvin Crane, weeks would pass before he could use his left arm again.

"Don't look so glum about it," Calvin told Nat. "Think about Cuffey and Toby, back in the *Alert* and off to do battle with old cannon and defective powder."

Both rogues had been unconscious after Israel had finished with them. Some passing shipmates had seen them lying in the road near the café and had carried them back aboard ship. It was too bad, though, that the *Alert* had sailed before her captain could be warned about the defective armaments.

As the morning wore on the gentle breeze gradually died away. By early afternoon the air was still and the convoy and privateers alike were becalmed. The *Dauntless* yawed sluggishly in the long oily swells which came surging out of the southeast.

Duff, popping out of his galley, glanced at the sky and sniffed. "Looks like a big twister coming," he said. "Those whirly cyclones always blow after a clear day when the air gets sticky-like. You see those little fluffs of clouds that look like cotton? If they don't blow off pretty quick, we're in for some weather."

The cottony cirrus clouds did not blow away. By dusk they were spreading, fanning upward to screen out the sunset. The night was starless.

At dawn a dense gray overcast blanketed the sky. A gusting wind began to blow and soon the sea became freckled with whitecaps.

Breakfast over, Nat went aft. Captain Beeler, pacing near the binnacle, ordered the boy to stand by to serve as messenger in the event of action. A few moments later Banty Spooner came down from aloft.

"Convoy's separating some, Cap'n," he reported. "Looks as if they're trying for some northing to get clear of the storm center."

"I reckoned they would." The captain stared intently at the horizon. "This storm will pass us by, Mr. Spooner. Still, we'll get some weather. Just enough, I hope."

Nat knew what the captain meant. Caught in the middle of the storm track, the brig would have all she could do to battle the elements. However, with only a good stiff blow to contend with, the *Dauntless* could attend to the important business of picking up stragglers from the convoy.

The sky grew darker as the hours passed. The wind began moaning eerily through the rigging. The *Dauntless*, her canvas stripped down, edged closer to the convoy. The British merchant squadron was bearing to the north in a wide arc, gradually taking more and more sea room as the weather worsened.

The afternoon was half gone when the lookouts reported two merchant vessels trailing along far in the rear of the escorting British frigate. Captain Beeler went aloft himself with his telescope. When he descended, he called the first officer and said quietly, "Call all hands, Mr. Spooner."

Canvas slatting, the *Dauntless* came about and streaked for the tail of the convoy. A heavy rain squall, sweeping across the sea, drenched the brig and cut visibility to a few hundred feet.

With the passing of the squall Nat could see the convoy plainly. The merchant squadron was scattered haphazardly. Briggs, brigantines, schooners, and ships dotted the sea as far as the eye could see. Some of the vessels were huge, ponderous craft, designed for cargo-carrying rather than for speed.

"Yon's the shepherd, Nat." Israel pointed over the starboard beam at a large black and yellow ship-rigged vessel. "Reckon he'll have some trouble watching his flock today."

Nat stared at the huge frigate. He had seen several like her in Boston Harbor during the British occupation. She was a two-decker, mounting at least fifty cannon and manned by a crew of at least five hundred men.

The frigate lay between the main fleet of merchantmen and the two slowpokes reported by the lookouts. She was hove to as though her commander couldn't decide just what to do. Without doubt, though, he was watching all three privateers, determined that they would take no prizes from his flock if he could help it.

Far beyond the frigate the privateer *Carnation* could be seen as she ran toward one of the laggards. The other privateer, *Yankee*, was a tiny speck in the distance as she sought to cut out the other straggler.

Blue-black smoke blossomed from the frigate followed by the thundering roar of her guns.

"The bulldog knows those privateers are out of range," Israel Boone commented, "but he's hoping to frighten 'em off."

Nat sighed. "If only there were more than two stragglers." he said. "As it is, the *Carnation* and *Yankee* will make prizes of them and we'll get nothing."

Israel grinned. "Don't fret, Nat. Cap'n Beeler knows what he's about. Those fellers"—he nodded toward the privateers—"are green as grass at this game. They ought to separate more and attack one at a time so's to keep the bulldog running from one to the other."

The frigate did no more firing. Instead, she came around, her great span of canvas filling as she went after the *Carnation* and *Yankee*. That was when Reddy Malone came aft, saying, "That bulldog skipper knows what he's about. He's chasing those other privateers and holding a course so he can watch us at the same time."

Israel chuckled. "He ain't so smart. If he was he'd have his weather eye peeled, like Cap'n Beeler."

The captain of the *Dauntless* was squinting into the southeast where a black rainsquall was racing across the sea toward the brig. Presently he turned and snapped, "That squall will hide us pretty quick, Mr. Spooner. When it does, we'll wear ship and run with it as long as we can." Stumping to the binnacle, he ordered, "Steady as she goes." Then: "Hands about ship." The boatswain's whistle piped.

The *Dauntless* held her course until the drenching gray curtain of rain closed in around her, then:

"Ease down the helm."

"Slack lee braces."

"Rise tacks and sheets."

The brig came around, topsails shaking, and then, shrouded by the downpour, she sped away to the northwest before the wind.

When the squall finally outran the brig, Nat gasped. The frigate was far astern, barely visible on the horizon. He could well imagine the British captain's consternation. He must have seen a Colonial privateer vanish in the squall. When he saw her again, minutes later, she was miles away, and heading in the opposite direction.

Banty Spooner lowered his telescope and chuckled. "The bulldogs putting about again, Cap'n. Reckon he's decided he'll let the stragglers go so he can protect his main fleet."

"Good," said the captain grimly. "Now, let's pick ourselves a prize."

Israel nudged Nat. "See what I mean, lad, about the skipper knowing his business? The *Carnation* and *Yankee* will get their prizes, and so will we."

Captain Beeler took the spyglass and leveled it on a large schooner off to starboard of the merchant fleet. "She'll do," he growled. "She's a smart sailer and a small prize crew shouldn't have much trouble getting her clear of the bulldog in this weather."

The *Dauntless* cracked on, standing toward the schooner. Before long Nat could read the name on her stern: *Apollo, Liverpool*.

The privateer ran up alongside the Britisher boldly, the Pine Tree Flag snapping out from the gaff and gunports flapping open. One of the *Dauntless'* forward guns roared, sending a shot across the schooner's bows.

Men were running back and forth on the schooner's decks. A few clustered around a small deck gun and for a few moments it looked as if the *Apollo* would show some fight. However, the British captain thought twice about risking a broadside from the *Dauntless'* eighteen-pounders.

"She's striking!" someone yelled as the British flag came fluttering down in a token of surrender. A triumphal cheer went up from the privateer's crew.

The *Dauntless* had taken her first prize.

"Get a boarding party aboard her, Mr. Spooner," the captain ordered crisply. "Send back her papers and any specie along with the prisoners. Lively now. We've no time to lose."

Nor was there. The big square sails of the frigate were growing rapidly.

The longboat was lowered into the turbulent sea. As it pulled away toward the *Apollo* Captain Beeler ordered Nat to fetch a quartermaster named Rooney. The captain appointed Rooney prize master of the captured schooner and ordered him to choose a crew of six to take the *Apollo* to the nearest Colonial port.

Calvin Crane had come topside to watch the capture. "Seamanship!" he murmured admiringly. He stared at the longboat, already alongside the schooner, bobbing like a cork. "I never would have thought this capture possible."

Nat, also, was amazed at Captain Beeler's strategy and the speedy taking of the *Apollo*. In a matter of minutes the prisoners were brought aboard and locked in the forehold. Several small kegs of specie were hauled to the deck.

By the time the prize crew was aboard and making ready to sail, the big yellow and black frigate was perilously close. Before the *Dauntless* was under way again, the bulldog's cannon began to thunder. Her shot fell short, but for a while it looked as if she might come within range.

The *Apollo*, manned by the prize crew, slipped off into the murk. The *Dauntless* followed, showing the frigate a clean pair of heels just as a shot from the frigate splashed into the sea less than fifty yards from her stern.

Later Nat checked over the *Apollo's* cargo list. She carried a few muskets and cutlasses but most of her merchandise was general. Nevertheless she was a valuable prize and her cargo included many items sorely needed in the colonies.

Captain Beeler, however, wasn't content with one prize. The next morning the *Dauntless* was on the fringes of the convoy again. Before the day was out she had taken a brig and another schooner. Before the British merchant fleet reached the safety of the Windward Passage a total of five prizes had been captured and sent to Colonial ports with prize crews aboard.

"Man alive," chortled Reddy Malone, peering over Nat's shoulder at the inventories. "I reckon General Washington's eyes'll pop when he hears about all this stuff we captured for him."

"Don't forget, Reddy," Israel Boone said. "Those prizes got to reach safe ports and they've got to run the bulldog blockade to do it. I'm hoping, though, that that *Star of Scotland* we took yesterday gets through. She was chock-full of military stores."

CHAPTER FIFTEEN

L'Orient

THE *Dauntless* swung to her anchor cables in the roadstead of L'Orient, a busy French seaport on the Bay of Biscay. The estuary of the Blavet River, which composed the harbor, was crowded with French, Dutch, and Spanish coastal craft. Mingled with them lay a number of Colonial privateers, most of them flying the Pine Tree Flag of Massachusetts.

All of the Colonial vessels, including one from New Hampshire and another from Rhode Island, bore evidence of long months at sea. Nearly all displayed battle scars—shattered spars, gaps in bulwarks, and patched-up hulls. Like the *Dauntless* they were low on powder and shot and, because of the prizes they had sent in, short-handed.

Nat was in the *Dauntless'* cabin, finishing up his work. Nearby, at the table, sat Reddy Malone and Sailing Master Asa Widgeon, who were studying charts of the Irish Sea and the English Channel.

Asa Widgeon adjusted his spectacles. With a worried frown, he asked, "You really calc'late, Mr. Malone, that the captain intends to sail into these hostile waters?"

"Reckon he does, Asa," Reddy replied. "That is if he can get a full crew and some powder and shot."

"But these waters are alive with bulldogs. It—it would be tempting fate."

Reddy shrugged. "I agree. If I was skipper I'd stick to the Sugar Islands trade routes. But you ought to know the old man by now. He'd sail right up the Thames to London and blast Buckingham Palace if he thought he had a halfway chance of getting by with it."

The sailing master was still fretting about the dangers of British waters when Nat finished his list and started a letter to his aunt. He started by telling of the *Dauntless'* adventures since leaving Cap François; of the captures made, escapes from enemy warships, and storms encountered.

The voyage had been successful for the most part; only once had the brig run into real trouble.

Off the Azores, the barkentine *Devonshire* refused to strike her colors. A lucky shot from the Britisher had shattered the *Dauntless'* foremast, giving the enemy the advantage. She was finally taken but not before five men of the *Dauntless* had been killed and six others wounded. One of the six—the Negro, Ginger—was still under Calvin Crane's care.

Nat wrote:

> *"We are now down to a crew of less than twenty, but Israel and Banty Spooner have gone to Nantes to find sailors who want to fight against England."*

He went on to write that Captain Beeler was in Paris for a talk with Benjamin Franklin, now one of the American Commissioners in the French city.

"France still has a neutrality treaty with England and our privateers and warships are not supposed to come into French ports at all. But they come anyway and French officials look the other way."

Nat wrote that quite a few Colonial privateers had been captured in the Bay of Biscay and in English waters. Many privateersmen were in English prisons.

"Captain Beeler is hoping that Dr. Franklin can arrange to exchange some of the prisoners for English sailors who have been captured———"

Nat paused thinking: wouldn't it be fine if Jeremy happened to be among such exchanged prisoners.

When he finished the letter, Nat placed it in the leather pouch which would be entrusted to the American Commission in Paris. Sooner or later it would be aboard some vessel bound for the colonies.

Nat went on deck and stared shoreward pensively. His gaze went beyond L'Orient's fortifications and warehouses to the neat blue and white houses surrounded by gardens. His eyes lingered on a church spire which thrust toward fleecy clouds. It reminded him of Boston.

He would have liked nothing better than to visit the shipyard he could see not too far distant. However, none of the crew was allowed ashore. Even the officers had to obtain special permits before they could leave the ship. It was irksome being confined aboard, but more than that, it was a constant reminder that the colonies still had not won France as an ally.

Some bumboatmen ranged alongside trying to sell squid, eels, and shellfish to the crew. A seaman looked up from his job of polishing metalwork and said, "They've got newspapers for sale, too, Nat, but"—he grunted in disgust—"they're all printed in French."

"Calvin Crane can translate them—" Nat began.

"I know. I've listened to Doc Crane read. But these Frenchies don't seem to print anything but political news. I want to hear about what's happening back home. Any word from the colonies, Nat?"

Nat shook his head. Since he was a clerk and close to the captain he was asked the same question dozens of time each day. "Maybe the captain will have news when he comes back from Paris."

"Hope so." The seaman nodded toward some fishing craft standing in. Swarming over them were dozens of gray-white gulls. "Reminds a feller of home. Why, I'd give all the prize money I've got comin' if I could be back in Marblehead fishin' for cod and haddock."

Nat went on forward and down the companionway to the doctor's quarters where he found Calvin Crane bandaging Ginger's leg.

"How's the patient, Calvin?"

"The infection is under control, Nat." A note of pride tinged Calvin's voice.

Ginger grinned up from his straw mattress. "I'm not

154

going to lose my leg, Nat. I sure am grateful to the Doc here. Any other ship's sawbones would have chopped that leg clean off instead of working on it so hard to heal it." He looked at Calvin fondly. "How long before I'll be walking, Doc?"

"Don't be impatient, Ginger. I'm having the carpenter make you a pair of crutches. Chips tells me they'll be ready in a few days."

"Crutches!" Ginger groaned. "You mean I have to walk with old sticks? How can I lay guns and fight bulldogs if'n I——"

"Only for a few weeks," Calvin assured him. "When the fracture knits you can throw the crutches away." He went on with his work, whistling softly.

Calvin had surely changed, Nat mused. Although he was still bitter over what had happened in Falmouth, he was no longer filled with hatred. Now, nothing was more important to him than caring for the sick and wounded. Saving a crushed limb which most surgeons would have unhesitatingly amputated meant more to him than vengeance upon an enemy.

Footsteps pounded on the deck overhead. A hoarse shout drifted down: "Privateer, standing in."

"Another Colonial vessel arriving, Nat," Calvin said. "She may have news if she's fresh from the colonies. Shall we go topside?"

Nat was none too hopeful. He knew that most of the privateers, after outfitting in the West Indies, spent many maurauding months at sea before reaching European ports.

The newly arrived craft was a trim, fast sloop. Watching her skim in across the placid estuary, Nat knew that he had seen that rakish mast and sleek hull before. Then, suddenly, he exclaimed, "She's the *Starlight* out of Beverly. Remember her, Calvin? We saw her when we were in the *Lee* with Captain Manley."

Crews lined the rails of the privateers in the harbor as the *Starlight* sped toward the anchorage, shedding her canvas as gracefully as a macaroni dandy doffing his hat to a lady. The afternoon sun glinted on her brightwork as she swung close to the *Dauntless* and her anchor rattled down. A tall man, his head wrapped with a red bandanna, appeared aft. Cupping his hands he shouted:

"Ahoy the *Dauntless*. Cap'n Beeler aboard?" He was Captain Lemon.

Reddy Malone was shouting back: "He's in Paris, Cap'n Lemon. Due back any day now. You fellers come straightaway from the colonies?"

"Right you are, mate. Twenty-five days out of Boston. Picked up two prizes on the way and——"

The rest of Captain Lemon's words were lost in the crew's thunderous barrage of questions. What's the news, Cap'n? What's going on in the colonies? Did General Washington hold New York? Got any letters for us?"

The *Starlight's* captain shook his head despairingly and held up a hand for silence. When the shouting subsided he yelled, "Some of us'll be aboard right off and give you the news." He turned and headed for the sloop's waist where some seamen were making ready to lower a small boat.

"Nat," Calvin pointed to the *Starlight*. "Isn't that one of our shipmates from the *Lee*? He was in the same gun crew with you——"

"Sure enough," Nat exclaimed. He raised his voice and waved an arm. "Joe," he shouted. "Joe Patch."

Joe Patch waved back. "Be right aboard you, Nat."

Within ten minutes Captain Lemon was clambering aboard the *Dauntless*. Behind him came Joe Patch and several seamen who were immediately surrounded by eager questioners.

"Prize money?" Joe Patch repeated when he was queried by a seaman. He settled down on a hatch cover and nodded. "Yep, I reckon you fellers got some prize money coming. Leastwise a couple of them prizes you took reached Boston. Saw 'em myself——"

"We took more than a couple," another man said.

"Maybe they got into other ports. Anyway, you couldn't expect all of 'em to get in safe with all those bulldogs patrollin' the coast." He shook his head. "The royal tyrant's sending more and more warships and troops to the colonies all the time—" he broke off and looked at Nat. "Where's Israel and Banty?"

"Off looking for seamen," Nat replied. "We're short-handed, just like the rest of the privateers here in L'Orient."

Joe Patch sighed. "Well, if it isn't one thing then it's something else. Now me, I joined the regular navy after I got mustered out of the *Lee*. Went down to Rhode Island where Commodore Hopkins had his Colonial squadron. Trouble was, Hopkins' fleet was all bottled up in Narragansett Bay by the bulldogs. I was lucky though. I got in a ship commanded by Cap'n John Paul Jones and I saw plenty of action."

"But wasn't he bottled up too?" Nat asked.

"Sure he was, but John Paul Jones is a real fighting skipper. Blockading squadrons, even commanded by a bulldog admiral like 'Black Dick' Howe didn't worry him any. We slipped right out past 'em——"

Joe Patch told how he had sailed in the *Providence* and *Alfred* with John Paul Jones and took dozens of prizes all the way from the Sugar Islands to the icy seas off Newfoundland. He ended up saying, "I wouldn't sail under anybody but him if I could help it."

"Then why didn't you stay with him, Joe?" Calvin asked.

Joe shrugged his shoulders. "After we put into Boston with a flock of prizes we took up north, that Marine Committee they've got in Congress kicked Cap'n Jones off his ship and refused to give him another." He shook his head dolefully. "Them politicians. There's just no understanding some of 'em. Anyway, since Cap'n Jones was on the beach, I signed in the *Starlight* as bos'n."

"What about Captain Manley, Joe?" Nat asked. "Did he ever take the new frigate *Hancock* to sea?"

"Yep. Sailed north in her last I heard. But except for the *Hancock* and a couple of others, the rest of the new frigates are sealed up in the places where they were built, snugger than herrings in a barrel. The way our navy's going, I reckon it's up to us privateers to knock out Redcoat commerce on the high seas."

"How about the war on land, Joe?"

Joe Patch took a deep breath. "It isn't any too good either. The patriots got booted out of New York——" He related how General Washington retreated through New Jersey and across the Delaware River. "Things looked right bad until General Washington outsmarted Cornwallis and captured a lot of Hessians at Trenton. Still . . ."

Joe reported that according to the Boston *Gazette,* just before the *Starlight* sailed, Congress was still at Baltimore, fearful that Philadelphia might be taken by the British.

"What about these Frenchies?" he asked. "They going to help us out or not? That's what folks keep asking back in the colonies."

"Well, Joe," said Calvin Crane, "according to the French papers I've been reading, the Prime Minister of France, and King Louis himself, want to give aid to the colonies. With Benjamin Franklin in Paris, I wouldn't be surprised if France were to declare an open alliance with us."

"Ben Franklin, eh?" Joe nodded. "I've heard of him. He's the fellow who wrote *Poor Richard's Almanack.* He's an inventor, too, I heard, as well as a writer."

"And a diplomat," Calvin added. "Congress couldn't have made a wiser choice when they decided to send him to the French court to plead the American cause. Dr. Franklin is probably the greatest diplomat in the world."

The next morning Nat noticed a number of strange faces among the crew at breakfast. Evidently Israel and Banty had been successful in recruiting men for the

Dauntless. Most were French, to judge by the names Nat was adding to the crew list, although there were a few Spaniards, Italians, and Dutchmen.

"Easy enough to find Frenchmen and Spaniards wanting to fight with us," Israel told Nat. " 'Specially if they've been cooped up in one of those British prisons like a lot of 'em have. Nothing worse than a British jail."

Early that afternoon Captain Beeler returned from Paris and called a conference of the privateering captains in L'Orient. Looking around at the assemblage in his cabin, he said:

"The situation here in France is still mighty ticklish accordin' to Dr. Franklin. Every time us privateers, or any Colonial men-o'-war, put into a French port, that British consul, Lord Stormont kicks up a big fuss. France isn't anxious for another war with England so she has to move careful-like."

Captain Lemon of the *Starlight* spoke up. "Stormont must know that we're getting guns and powder in the French islands."

"Sure he knows," Captain Beeler said drily, "but there's not much he can do because the armaments are being sold to us by private interests. The French can't outfit us here unless it's done on the sly. Stormont's seen to that. He's kept 'em from setting up prize courts too. We won't get any direct help from France until she comes right out and declares for the colonies."

"Think she'll do it?" one of the captains asked.

"Dr. Franklin thinks so, but he's not sure when. Anyway, there's no point in our roosting here and waiting. We got to go out and fight."

"And if we do," Captain Lemon asked, "what do we do with our prizes?"

"Same as the rest of us have been doing," was the reply. "You've got to deal with French merchants who'll take 'em off your hands when nobody's looking."

"And offer you about half what they're worth," a black-bearded Boston skipper growled.

Captain Beeler grinned. "You haven't done so badly, Zeb. Maybe the French can drive a hard bargain, but so can Yankee horse-traders like us. As I see it, our job is to keep on grabbing British cargo ships. The more the better. I've heard that marine insurance rates are sky-rocketing in England and the merchants are howling blue murder to bring the war to an end. So, let's keep at 'em——"

"But how can we?" another captain asked. "I got hardly more'n a bar'l of powder left——"

"Maybe that's enough. Maybe you can capture what powder you need. It's taking a chance, I admit, but we got to take chances if we expect to lick England. Folks back in the colonies are taking chances every day. They're having to make do with whatever they got—and they haven't got much. I aim to do the same thing at sea. This brig of mine is sailing with the tide in the morning —and sailing smack into the Irish Sea."

CHAPTER SIXTEEN

The Lion's Jaws

SHAPING A COURSE midway between Cape Clear and the Scilly Islands, the *Dauntless* stood in through St. George's Channel to the Irish Sea. She ran up the English coast toward the Isle of Man, taking two prizes on the way. A Scottish brig, deep-laden with grain, was captured off Whitehaven; an English schooner with a cargo of linen surrendered without a struggle.

Circling back, the brig headed southward again, hugging close to the Irish coast. Off Dublin she spoke the Colonial privateer *Oliver Cromwell*, whose captain bawled a warning:

"Keep an eye skinned for bulldogs, Cap'n Beeler. Three or four of 'em in these waters, sloops-of-war and frigates. They aim to clear the Irish Sea of us privateers."

As Captain Beeler stumped below, he chuckled and said, "Reckon the English are getting a mite nervous. They never did expect us to raid their commerce within eyesight of their homeland."

"But look here, Cap'n." Asa Widgeon looked up from his charts and jerked at his pigtail nervously. "This sea is like a British lake, and we're sailing in it with hardly enough powder aboard to bring down a duck. Sooner or later one of those bulldogs will sight us and——"

"Reckon you're right, Asa, for once," Captain Beeler conceded. "Calculate we'll head for Bilbao. There's a chance we might pick up powder and shot at that Spanish port. If not, then we'll dog the westbound convoys for the Sugar Islands and head home for a refitting."

The next morning, blown by a stiff southwest breeze, the *Dauntless* was running out of the Irish Sea past Cape Clear when Nat heard the lookout's muffled shout:

"Sail ho! Larb'd bow."

Captain Beeler rose and started for the companion. Behind him came Asa Widgeon, saying, "We'd best be careful, Cap'n. We're so short on powder——"

"You said that before Asa," the captain snapped. "I reckon we've enough left to take another prize if we get the chance."

"But——"

"If all the privateer captains went pussyfooting around the way you admire, Asa, the British would have little to worry about, and the colonies never would get their independence." As he started up the ladder, he called back over his shoulder. "Nat, bring along my telescope. Asa gets me so jumpy I wonder I don't forget my own name."

On deck the captain called to the lookout, "What do you make of her?"

"She's ship-rigged, sir," came the reply from aloft. "Headed north. She looks like one of those big British East Indiamen."

At this some of the crew cheered. An East Indiaman, inbound, would surely carry a rich cargo from the Orient: silks, spices, ivory, chinaware, and tea. Perhaps even jewels and gold.

Glancing out over the choppy sea Nat could barely see the topsails of the big stranger.

Banty Spooner and Israel Boone came running aft. Banty took the telescope and clambered aloft. After a few moments he shouted, "A clumsy sailer, sir. Looks like an Indiaman, all right."

"And if that's what she is, Cap'n," Israel said, "she'll have been at sea for quite a spell. Maybe she won't even know the colonies are at war with England."

Captain Beeler nodded and gave an order to the helmsman. The *Dauntless* veered and squared away on a course that would take her past the stranger's stern yet at a safe distance.

A half-hour later the big vessel could be clearly seen. She was wallowing along slowly as though tired after a long voyage.

"She's bound for the Channel," said Israel. "Likely headed for Plymouth or——"

"Cap'n, I don't like this," Asa Widgeon interrupted sharply. "She's too big. Why, she'd make four of us. If she carries any guns——"

"She won't have much in the way of arms, Asa," said Israel. "Those Indiamen carry some cutlasses and pistols maybe, and some swivels to fight off the Malay pirates in the Sunda Straits. Nothing that'll bother us any."

"I still don't like it," the sailing master protested. "We've taken enough chances already. We——"

"Pipe down, Asa," Captain Beeler roared. "How in

164

Tophet can I think with your infernal prattling!" He lifted the glass and aimed it at the square-rigger. "Only a few men on deck," he muttered as if to himself. "No gunports that I can see." He turned to Banty. "What's your opinion, Mr. Spooner?"

"Reckon she's an Indiaman," Banty replied. "Looks like she's had a long, hard voyage."

"And you, Mr. Boone?"

Israel stroked his jaw thoughtfully. "Wal, Cap'n, there's always a chance that a man-o'-war might be fixed up to look like a merchantman. However, the British haven't ever been too partial to such tricks that I know of."

"There's always a first time," Asa Widgeon declared. "I——"

"For the last time, Asa, stow it!" The captain studied the plodding stranger intently for a few moments, then: "Beat to quarters, Mr. Spooner. We're taking her."

"Aye aye, sir."

At the shrill of the boatswain's whistle, Nat dashed to his station. With the crew short-handed he had been assigned to number three gun whenever the brig was about to go into action. His job was to bring up powder and shot, matches, sand buckets, and other gear from below.

Absalom, captain of number three, grinned broadly when Nat reported. "I sure hope that fellow fights a little, Nat," he said. "We need some practice with this cannon."

"We won't get much, Ab," said Nat. "We've about enough powder for three or four rounds."

The rest of the gun crew came running on the dou-

165

ble. One of them, a stocky seaman named Belial Crump, said, "Let's get her unlimbered, Ab. If we take that Indiaman, we'll be rolling in gold." The others in the crew —three Frenchmen who had joined the *Dauntless* at L'Orient—smiled with anticipation.

By the time the shot racks were filled and the slow matches burning in the sand tubs, the stranger was less than a mile off. She maintained her course, sailing slowly along as if unaware of any danger.

As the distance lessened, Nat realized how big the stranger was. "Man alive, she's huge!" he muttered under his breath. He could see the Union Jack at her masthead. On her stern were some blocked letters but they were so weathered and apparently encrusted with salt, they couldn't be read.

Banty Spooner strode forward, barking, "Break out the langrage and chain shot, boys. If they decide to fight for it, we'll rip the sails out of her and cut her rigging to pieces."

Nat ran to fetch the langrage—bags containing bolts, nails, glass, and other scrap which would wreak havoc with an enemy's canvas. Chain shot consisted of two iron balls connected with a piece of chain. It could be sent whirling through the air to cut rigging and bring down spars.

The *Dauntless* tacked and, with the stranger under her lee, ran closer.

"Up with the Pine Tree Flag," Captain Beeler shouted. "Number one stand ready to put a warning shot over his bows."

Nat couldn't keep his eyes off the enormous black

ship. He could see men on her deck. They appeared to be looking curiously at the little privateer. One was pointing to the Pine Tree Flag.

"Fire number one."

The eighteen-pounder belched smoke and flame as, with a roar, it sent a shot across the stranger's bows.

Nat was staring at the stranger's flag, wondering when it would be hauled down. Then, his eyes widened as he noticed a white bundle start to go up the stranger's signal halyard. As it reached the masthead, unfolded and rippled out in the wind, a sudden hush came over the crew of the *Dauntless*.

Nat heard Belial Crump say in a kind of croaking voice, "Yon—yon's the White Ensign. She—she's a bulldog!"

Nat did not have to be told. He had seen the emblem of the Royal Navy often enough in Boston.

"We're done for," Crump was moaning. As he spoke, a row of gunports along the black ship's hull flapped open and the glinting muzzles of huge cannon snouted out.

The *Dauntless* had blundered into a trap. Instead of a rich East Indiaman, the little brig was confronted by a British sloop-of-war. She'd mount over twenty cannon which could blow the *Dauntless* to bits with a single broadside.

"Run out the guns," came the order from aft.

Faintly Nat could hear Asa Widgeon's shrill cry, "But, Captain, we can't fight her. We'll have to surrender or be sent to the bottom——"

"We'll not strike," the captain shouted. "If we can

167

cut her tophamper and rigging we might get clear——"

"Br-ooom!" A shattering roar resounded, and the brig shuddered as if struck by a giant's sledge hammer. A crunching, rending sound came from forward as a shot tore through wood and scattered murderous splinters in all directions. Screams of agony pierced the air.

"Fire," the captain ordered. "Aim high. Fire on the uproll."

"Br-oo-m!" Number five fired. Absalom poured powder into the touch hole of number four and applied the slow match. Whoosh! Flame flared up along the trickle of powder, then: "Br-oo-m!"

Nat thought he saw a ragged hole appear in the enemy's mizzen topsail but he couldn't be sure. There wasn't time for observation now. It was swab, load, and fire, this time with langrage.

"Br-oom!" Number three sent out a cloud of scrap metal which screamed toward the Britisher, ripping her foretopsail almost to shreds.

Banty Spooner yelled, "Load chain shot. Aim for her rigging."

Half-blinded and almost suffocated by the acrid smoke, Nat struggled with the shot. The cannonading was almost continuous, but over its thunder he could hear the rattle of musketry as the sharpshooters in each vessel tried to bring down seamen who were aloft. Then, as he leaned over the shot rack, all sounds merged into an ear-splitting blast, and he felt himself hurled across the deck.

Stunned, he lay still for a few seconds. Israel's "You all right, Nat?" brought him to his feet. Where num-

ber three had been was a gaping hole. The gun itself had been shot clear of its lashings. It was lurching crazily on the deck and some seamen were trying to help Belial Crump secure it. Nat saw Absalom leaning over two of the Frenchmen who were prone on the deck, moaning softly.

"Nat," said Israel, "lend a hand getting the wounded below, then report aft."

"Yes, sir." Nat helped carry one of the Frenchmen to the doctor's quarters, which was now jammed with wounded. Calvin Crane, stripped to the waist, looked up from a wailing patient. "Put him on the floor with the others, Nat. I'll get to him in a while."

Nat looked at Calvin with wonder. It seemed unbelievable that Calvin could remain so calm in that sick bay full of terribly injured men. And he was treating them swiftly and capably too. As Nat left, he noticed the knives and a saw on a bench. He shuddered, realizing there would be arms and legs that even Calvin could not hope to save this day. Lives, too, for that matter!

Reaching the deck again, Nat staggered as another murderous broadside slammed into the brig. Something crackled aloft and, glancing up, he saw the top foremast slowly leaning backward. The crackling grew louder and Nat ran, barely escaping the falling tangle of spars, canvas, and rigging.

Hurrying aft, Nat saw Captain Beeler slumped against the binnacle, his hand pressed to his side. Asa Widgeon was crying frantically, "We must strike, Captain. The foremast has gone by the boards. We're completely out of powder. We'll all be killed——"

The captain's lips moved but no words came. Suddenly he slumped to the deck and lay still.

The sailing master knelt by his commander's side for a moment. Then, with a harsh sob, he leaped to his feet. "I—I must do it," he muttered as he made his way to the signal halyard.

A sick, empty feeling came over Nat. His eyes filled as he saw the Pine Tree Flag come tumbling down to lay in a desolate little pile on the deck.

The *Dauntless* had struck her colors.

CHAPTER SEVENTEEN

Old Mill

A DENSE GRAY FOG rolled in from the English Channel and enshrouded the town of Plymouth. The chill mist swirled about the company of privateersmen who, flanked by armed guards, plodded along a winding, rutty road toward Old Mill Prison.

Nat Harkins, his shoulders slumped, trudged wearily between Calvin Crane and Asa Widgeon. He was thinking about the talk he had heard from men who had been confined in English jails: poor food and mighty little of it; foul air and sickness——

"Straighten up, Nat," came a booming voice from behind. Israel Boone put a hand on the boy's shoulder. "Things might be worse."

Nat lifted his head. Israel was right. Why, he might have been badly wounded like Captain Beeler, Reddy Malone, Duff, and all the others who were in a hospital somewhere. He might have been one of the many who had been killed.

"We might get out before too long, Nat," Israel

went on. "Ben Franklin's working to fix things so's we can be exchanged."

"If we're not," clacked Banty Spooner, "we'll get out of Old Mill some other way."

One of the guards, hearing this, brandished his bayoneted musket and growled, "Planning to escape, be ye? Even before you're locked up! Keep on with that kind of gab and you'll find yourselves in the Black 'Ole."

Lapsing into silence, the prisoners shuffled on toward the massive stone wall which loomed ahead in the fog. Nat could see several figures carrying muskets pacing along the top of the structure.

When they stopped in front of a huge iron gate, the sergeant of the guards reported to the armed sentries, "Rebels from the Yankee pirate ship *Dauntless*. Found guilty of piracy, rebellion, and high treason at the King's Court in Plymouth this morning."

"Herd 'em inside," one of the sentries drawled. "The warden will make them welcome." He grinned and winked. "Show them to the royal quarters. Nothing's too good for rebels, I always say."

Prodded by bayonets the prisoners were hustled through the entrance toward another stone wall patrolled by more sentries. With a creak the inner gate swung open to reveal a dimly lit room where some prison officials were seated at a table.

"Here are some special birds, warden," the sergeant of guards said. "These are the pirates who tried to fight the Royal Navy's sloop-of-war *Falcon*."

"A likely-looking lot." The long-nosed, gray-bearded warden surveyed the group with piercing blue eyes.

"Line them up, Sergeant. Have them strip and search them for concealed weapons. After that the clerk will take their names and descriptions." He stalked out.

Nat, his clothes off, stood shivering while a clerk wrote down his name and then inspected him for marks. "H'm. Six-inch scar on the left shoulder—" he muttered, writing in his book. "That'll be useful if you escape and we have to post a description. That'll be all, 'Arkins. Put on your clothes."

After all the prisoners had been searched and booked, the sergeant barked, "Into the next room, all of you. You'll get your gear at the counter."

Nat fell into line behind Israel and, as they reached the counter, the big seaman drawled, "Wal, if I'm not a cross-eyed grampus, Nat! What'll these lobsterbacks think of next! Imagine—setting a polecat to issuing blankets and such!"

"Watch your language, you big loon, or you'll find yourself in the Black Hole."

Nat stiffened, hearing the familiar voice. The clerk behind the counter was Seth Cuffey. Plainly, the privateer *Alert* had been captured and her crew imprisoned and Cuffey had somehow wormed himself into the good graces of the warden.

Israel looked around. "I don't see your mate, hereabouts, Cuffey. What happened to Toby?"

"He—" Cuffey clamped his jaws together.

"He's dead, likely," Israel regarded Cuffey narrowly. "Reckon he might have been killed when one of those old cannon you got in Cap François blew up, eh?"

Seth's eyes flickered but he quickly regained his com-

174

posure. "I don't know what you're talking about." Then, seeing Nat, he grinned. "Well, if it isn't my old mate, Nat Harkins." He gave a mock bow. "Welcome to Old Mill, sir. We trust you'll find the accommodations to your liking and that you'll be with us for quite a spell." He reached back into a rack and selected two threadbare blankets which he threw at Nat and Israel.

"See here," Israel growled. "These blankets aren't fit for a dog."

"Maybe not," Cuffey smirked. "But they're plenty good enough for the likes of you."

"Why, you puffed-up, miserable turncoat." Israel leaned over the counter threateningly. "I'll———"

"Move on," shouted the sergeant of guards. "Get them blankets and mess gear issued, Cuffey. We haven't got all day."

The line of prisoners moved on, filing through another gate toward a big square stone building in the center of the prison yard. The sergeant unlocked the door and swung it open. "In with ye."

Nat found himself in an enormous stone room studded here and there with a few small windows that let in hardly any light. Only the faint glow of the candles revealed the many prisoners in the place. Most of them were stretched out on the floor. The few who were sitting up mending clothes glanced indifferently at the newcomers, their pale faces without expression.

Mill Prison, Nat was thinking, was as awful as he had been told. His nose wrinkled at the sour, stale reek of the air. He tried not to listen to the racking coughs as he stood with his shipmates, looking around uncertainly.

An erect figure emerged from the shadows and strode toward the newcomers. Something about him raised Nat's spirits. He didn't look beaten down like the rest. His blue uniform, despite its raggedness, was somehow neat and clean. His straw-colored hair was carefully tied in a pigtail with a bit of twine. His eyes were bright and, despite the bleak surroundings, he seemed in good spirits.

Singling out Israel Boone, the young man offered his hand. "I'm Richard Dale," he said. "Until lately, midshipman of the Colonial naval brig *Lexington*. You're the *Dauntless'* men, aren't you?"

"Right you are, Dale," Israel replied. "How'd you know?"

Dale laughed lightly. "We have means of getting information here at Old Mill. Come along, all of you. I've arranged floor space." He led the way, stepping agilely over prone figures as he took them to the far end of the vast room. "Here we are."

Pointing to an unoccupied area, he said, "Pick yourselves a few feet of floor and set up housekeeping. You'll spend your time in here except during the day when we have the freedom of the inner yard." He was glancing at Nat as he spoke. "Haven't we met somewhere before?" he asked.

Nat shook his head. He was sure that if ever he had met Richard Dale he would not have forgotten him.

"I'd have sworn—" Dale frowned thoughtfully. Then, he noticed Calvin Crane who was feeling the pulse of a man who was groaning softly. "Is he a doctor?"

"Not exactly," Calvin himself replied. "However, I served as ship's surgeon in the *Dauntless*."

176

"Good. We'll have use for you here."

"But, without medicines——"

"We'll have medicines," Dale assured him. "We have ways of getting such things, despite the prison authorities." Again he turned to Nat. "Do you happen to hail from Boston?" As Nat nodded, he went on. "And is it possible that your name is Harkins? Nat Harkins?"

"That's right," Nat looked puzzled. "But——"

Richard Dale smiled. "I've heard all about you, Nat. Come along with me."

Taking Nat's arm, he guided him toward one of the thick columns which supported the ceiling. Lying on a blanket at the base of the column was a thin, still figure.

"Your brother Jeremy," Dale said softly. "At least

what's left of him after forty days in the Black Hole. But don't worry, Nat. We'll bring Jeremy around. He'll be fit as a fighting cock in a few weeks."

At the sound of Dale's voice, Jeremy opened his eyes and half rose. He blinked, then said hoarsely, "Nat! But it can't be . . . I—I must be dreaming."

"You're not dreaming, Jeremy." Nat knelt down beside his brother. "It's me all right. I was in the *Dauntless* and——"

"You should have stayed home, Nat, to build ships——"

"I couldn't do that. Not while there was fighting to do." A lump came to his throat when he saw his brother's pallid, hollow-cheeked face and his swollen, infected wrists cut by manacles.

"Jeremy's been cruelly treated," Richard Dale said. "You see, he almost succeeded in escaping."

"Almost," Jeremy murmured weakly. "I—I smuggled myself out in a coffin, Nat. Took the place of a prisoner who died. I reached Plymouth and rode the coach to Southampton, bold as brass."

In Southampton, Jeremy was sheltered by an Englishman sympathetic to the American cause. His passage to France in a fishing boat was arranged.

"We were close to Morlaix when a British patrol schooner challenged us. I tried to swim to shore but—I'd have made it if I wasn't so weak." He shrugged his thin shoulders.

"Punishment for attempted escape," Richard Dale said, "is confinement in the Black Hole."

"I've been hearing about that place," Nat said. "I——"

178

"No matter what you've heard," Dale said bitterly, "you couldn't imagine what the place is like. It's an underground dungeon, black as the inside of a chimney flue. You're thrown in, arms and legs in irons. Now and then a guard tosses you a crust of bread which the rats try to get away from you when they aren't gnawing at your toes. Many a man has died in the Black Hole or has had his spirit broken completely."

Nat, looking into his brother's eyes, was thinking: he's suffered terribly, but he hasn't changed. He still has that fierce will to fight.

Jeremy propped himself up on one elbow. "What about you, Nat? How did you happen to sign in the *Dauntless?*"

"I suppose it all began with Seth Cuffey," Nat explained. "But for him I might not have gone off to sea with Israel Boone——"

When Nat mentioned the scuffle at the café in Cap François, Jeremy interrupted, "Old condemned guns. Defective powder. So that's why the *Alert* was taken by a puny British brig. No wonder her guns blew apart." He shook his head. "Cuffey told the prison authorities here that he was forced aboard the *Alert* in Cap François by a press gang, and that he was a true Loyalist. He's a powerful talker, Nat. Watch him while you're here in Old Mill."

Long before the first dreary month ended, Nat noticed that Richard Dale was continually searching the faces of the new arrivals. He turned from any who seemed abject or cowed. Those who had spirit he sought out and talked with in low tones.

One night he called a trusted group, including Nat, to the far end of the prison house to disclose what he had in mind.

"Escape, isn't it?" Israel asked. "I've been smelling it in the air."

Richard Dale smiled. "I've been thinking about it ever since I've been here, and have concluded that a simple plan is the best. We can dig a tunnel under both walls of the prison to the outside."

"A tunnel!" Asa Widgeon shook his head. "That's not practical, Dale. What do we use for picks and shovels? What do we do with the dirt we take out? Why, if the guards saw any loose piles of earth they would get suspicious right away."

"Widgeon's right," said a burly privateer captain. "Burrowing in the ground like a confounded gopher won't get us any place but into the Black Hole."

"Perhaps," Dale asked mildly, "you two have some other scheme in mind?"

When neither man spoke, Jeremy Harkins said, "I say let's try Dick's plan."

"But it would take months, maybe years," Asa Widgeon protested.

"Suppose it does?" Jeremy replied. "Suppose it takes two years? The fight for Independence will go on for longer than that or I miss my guess. We're not certain that Dr. Franklin can ever arrange to exchange prisoners. So as things stand now we have two choices. We can squat here and rot or——"

"What'll we use to dig with?" Banty Spooner asked.

"Sharpened sticks, spoons, our hands, anything." Richard Dale said. "As for getting rid of the dirt, we'll wash it down the drains or spread it around the grounds thinly. Maybe"—he grinned—"we'll have to eat it. But we'll get it out of sight one way or another."

"I'm with ye, Dale," said Banty. "All the way."

"Me, too," Israel Boone declared. "And the sooner we start the better I'll like it. Where do we start to dig, Dick? I reckon you've got the starting place picked out?"

CHAPTER EIGHTEEN

The Tunnel

THE GUARDS PACING the top of the ten-foot stone walls looked down indifferently at one of the prisoners who was trying to keep himself in good condition. Sometimes the prisoner would stretch his arms or lean down to touch his toes. Now and then he would trot or pace in a tight circle. The guards had no idea that the prisoner, Nat Harkins, was on watch.

Nat's eyes constantly ranged the main prison yard. Whenever a guard approached the corner where the tunnel was being dug, he would raise both arms high three times. This was the signal for another watcher to alert the diggers underground. In a matter of seconds they could emerge, place boards and stones over the hole, and thus conceal all evidence of the tunnel work.

Despite his exercising, Nat shivered. It was a cold day and a chill, drizzling rain fell constantly. He would be glad when it was his turn to dig again.

A few prisoners were out, some playing leapfrog or other games to keep warm. The only guards visible were those patrolling the walls.

A tall figure emerged from the prison house and ambled toward Nat. "Calvin," Nat called. "How are all the patients?"

"Some good, some bad, Nat." Calvin replied. "A medicine man is under handicaps here."

"But you're getting medicines, aren't you?"

"Yes. Dick has got some smuggled in through friends of the colonies in England. But he can't smuggle fresh air into that prison house." He lowered his voice. "Much progress with the tunnel, Nat?"

Nat shrugged. "It's slow work. Jeremy reckons that we're under the inside wall, but there's still a long distance to go."

Calvin nodded. "It's been four months since you started."

"The ground's so hard that it has to be chipped away," Nat explained. "Still, if it were soft, we would have cave-ins to worry about."

"And another problem," Calvin said, "is to get rid of the dirt?"

"Yes. We've been carrying it out in our pockets and scattering it over the grounds when the guards aren't watching. But there aren't many places left where we can throw it without them getting suspicious. We don't dare put too much down the drains. They might clog up and the officials would investigate——" He broke off, seeing a guard striding through one of the gates.

Nat began his exercising again. As the guard approached, he raised his arms high, three times.

The guard paused and grinned. "You blokes practicing to fly over the walls like birds?" He shook his head.

"Nothing you rebels won't try to get out of here. But you won't escape from Old Mill. We're onto all your tricks."

When the guard went on, Calvin said, "Nat, I think I have a way of getting rid of dirt from the tunnel——"

"You have? Tell me about it."

"I've had some patients down with fever and I've wanted to find a place to keep them separate from the others. I still haven't found an isolation ward, but I did locate a place where nobody would ever think of looking for anything."

Calvin explained that he had noticed a grating in the ceiling of the prison building. Thinking it might lead to an attic, he had investigated. "It was only a narrow space between the roof and ceiling. Just enough room to crawl in, but it covers a large area. You could hide tons of earth in there."

"A fine idea, Calvin!" Nat exclaimed. "We'll tell Jeremy and Dick about it."

That night, by flickering candlelight, the attic was investigated and decided upon as a hiding place for the excavated earth. Soon a ladder was improvised and kept hidden when not in use. Thereafter small amounts of earth, carried in the prisoner's pockets, were deposited nightly between the rafters.

The weeks passed, and the months, too, as with agonizing slowness the tunnel lengthened. Often Asa Widgeon was heard to say, "We'll never get through."

"Well, at least it gives us something to do," someone else would always say. At first the comment was offered jokingly but, as time went on, it was uttered in a dull, hopeless tone.

Seth Cuffey's announcements, too, lowered the men's spirits. "He seems to get real pleasure out of making us miserable," Dick Dale said one night.

Nat nodded. Cuffey occasionally joined the guards during their inspection rounds. Often he would pause to give out news of the war. He had told about Philadelphia being captured by the British. "And that's not all," he went on gleefully. "That slick new frigate, named after the rebel *Hancock,* has been grabbed by the Royal Navy's *Rainbow.* The whole blamed crew, including Cap'n Manley himself, are in the prison hulks at New York."

Israel rumbled wrathfully, "I reckon that polecat's lying to us."

Cuffey, however, had told the truth. A month later some captured privateersmen, fresh from the colonies, confirmed the fall of Philadelphia and the loss of the *Hancock.* "She was taken, right enough," said one of the privateersmen. "The British refitted her and named her the *Iris.* Saw her myself off Morlaix a few weeks back."

However, all the news wasn't bad. As the year of 1777 drew to a close, heartening tidings reached the prisoners of Old Mill. From English newspapers they learned that the British were becoming increasingly alarmed by the loss of their shipping. British merchants were complaining loudly and protesting against high insurance rates. Also, the privateers were becoming so bold that they were raiding seacoast villages.

Nor was that all. The invading British army, moving southward from Canada under General Burgoyne, had been stopped in its tracks. Nearly six thousand Redcoats and Hessians had been captured by the patriots.

"Fine news!" Calvin Crane exclaimed. "Now an alliance between France and the United Colonies is more than possible. By forcing Burgoyne's surrender, the patriots have shown their mettle to King Louis. It proves their motto, 'Liberty or Death,' is more than an idle phrase."

Within a few months Calvin's prediction came to pass. Word filtered into the prison that a great French fleet, under Count d'Estaing, was sailing for the colonies to bottle up the British at Philadelphia. From the columns of a British paper it was learned that the French treaty had been negotiated by Benjamin Franklin. France, pledging her aid, had acknowledged the independence of the United Colonies.

The prisoners went wild with joy. Now that the colonies had been recognized as a nation, the privateersmen could not be considered pirates and rebels. Men told each other, "England will have to treat us as prisoners of war now. We'll be exchanged for Redcoat prisoners. Ben Franklin'll see to it——"

Exchanged! The word resounded through the yard until the guards, attracted by the commotion, came on the run.

"Quiet now, you blinkin' rebels," a guard yelled. "Or you'll all be exchanging the yard here for the Black Hole."

Jeremy, who had done no cheering, said to Nat, "Maybe we'll be exchanged, but more likely we won't. Anyway we'll keep digging the tunnel, and someday we'll get out of here to fight again."

The weeks rolled by. If any headway was being made

in the negotiations for exchanging prisoners, the men in Old Mill could learn nothing about it. The pall of gloom which was always over the grim stoned jail seemed heavier than ever.

To Nat the spring of 1778 was the blackest time he had ever known. Like the rest of the prisoners he felt that he had been completely forgotten by the world outside the dank gray walls. And then, to increase the prisoners' despair tenfold, came the cave-in.

Nat was in the tunnel with Dick Dale when it happened. Both were scraping away with sharpened sticks, working with only the light of a guttering candle to guide them.

"Another few months, Nat," said Richard Dale, "and —hullo. The ground is getting softer."

"I noticed that too," Nat said. "It's damp, too."

"Probably an underground spring or seep. Let's hope —look out, Nat!"

They both lunged backward as a great slab of earth peeled from the top of the tunnel and fell with a rumble. It was some time before they could find the stub of candle and relight it.

Nat stared dismally at the cave-in—at months of work undone in seconds.

"We'll have to go back, Nat," said Richard Dale tonelessly. "We can't go through that wet place. We'll have to start again in another direction. It will take a great deal of time . . ."

CHAPTER NINETEEN

A Man Named Jones

ON A WARM NIGHT in the summer of 1778 Nat came into the prison house, climbed the ladder, and crawled out among the rafters to empty his pockets of dirt. Realizing how many tons of earth had accumulated under the roof, he wondered if the ceiling might not sag and thus betray the escape plan.

He mentioned the possibility to Jeremy during the evening meal, which consisted of hard crusts of bread and boiled bones with only a few shreds of tough meat and gristle on them.

Jeremy, who was cracking a bone on the stone floor to get at the marrow, glanced up at the ceiling. "It isn't sagging yet, Nat, and let's hope that it won't. Those timbers are mighty strong."

Just then Banty Spooner emerged from the shadows, a newspaper in his hand. "I got this from one of them fellers from the *Alert*," he said, hunching down. "Tells all about Cap'n John Paul Jones."

"John Paul Jones!" Nat exclaimed. "I remember Joe Patch telling us about him. Joe sailed with Captain Jones when he took a lot of prizes. The Marine Committee of Congress took away his command."

"Look's like he's got another ship now, Nat," Banty said with a chuckle. "And he's raising hob all around these British islands. It's all here in the London *Post*." He held the paper close to a flickering candle. "It says here, 'the pirate captain, John Paul Jones, in the pirate craft *Ranger*, is looting our coasts while the Royal Navy dawdles——' "

Banty went on reading. The newspaper account stated that the *Ranger* "impertinently" flying a flag with thirteen red and white stripes and thirteen stars, had put into the English seaport of Whitehaven on the Irish Sea. Captain Jones, going ashore with his men in small boats, had spiked the guns of the two forts guarding the harbor. After that he had set fire to the shipping at the wharves.

"Man alive!" Israel exclaimed. "He stepped right onto the King's soil under those guns?"

"He did that and more," Banty said. "Listen to this——"

After the daring raid on Whitehaven, Captain Jones sailed to the south of Scotland where he raided the estate of the famous Earl of Selkirk.

"He reckoned to capture the Earl and hold him for the exchange of Colonial prisoners like us in English prisons. Only the Earl was off gallivanting in London."

Richard Dale said, "That Captain Jones is a man after my own heart."

"And mine," Jeremy said. "I'd like nothing better than to sail with a skipper like——"

"Don't you want to hear the rest of it?" Banty snapped testily. "It says here that Jones got into a broadside battle with the British ship-of-war *Drake*. He shot her rigging to pieces and made her strike her colors. Then he took her into the French port of Brest as a prize of war."

"By golly," said Israel, "looks like Cap'n Jones has a good ship under him. He must have, to grab off that *Drake*."

"She's not much," a recently captured privateersman said. "I saw her being built for the Colonial navy at Portsmouth in New Hampshire. She wasn't much over a hundred feet long. Mounted eighteen six-pounders, if I remember right."

The exploits of Captain Jones were the talk of Old Mill Prison for days. Word even reached the prisoners that people in English coastal villages were fleeing inland with all their belongings.

Israel, hearing this, grunted with satisfaction. "The British folks are getting a taste of what the Colonists got at Falmouth."

In the weeks that followed, however, spirits drooped low again. Word filtered through that Captain Jones was in trouble with the French authorities over landing several hundred British prisoners. For some reason he was without a ship again.

During the remainder of the year and into the spring of 1779 the reports which came from the colonies were dismaying. The French fleet under Count d'Estaing had maneuvered in Colonial waters with little success, then departed for the West Indies. General Washington's patriots, camped in New Jersey facing the British who occupied New York, suffered continual losses. Savannah had been taken by the British. Indians, aroused by Tories, were burning and pillaging inland villages, tomahawking women and children.

In low spirits, Nat pecked away at the tunnel. Sometimes he believed that Asa Widgeon and some of the others were right. This grinding labor was as futile as the colonies' struggle for independence. One day he said morosely to his brother, "Jeremy, we've been digging this tunnel for nearly two years."

"And we'll keep on digging, Nat," Jeremy replied in a quiet voice. "We'll keep digging until we get out."

"Jeremy's right, Nat. We'll get out," Richard Dale said confidently. "When men make up their minds to do something, and have the will to keep on, the battle is more than half won."

The tunnel went on, inch by inch, foot by foot. Would the digging never end, Nat wondered. Surely they must be close to the outside by now.

And then, one afternoon, Dick Dale announced, "We're just about under the outer wall now. Next, we'll begin to slope upward. And carefully too. We don't want a hole showing outside that the guards could see from the walls. With any luck another month should see us out of here."

Escape! The word rippled on the lips of the prisoners who were in on the escape plot. A month. Thirty days. What was that? Nothing compared to the time they'd spent in Old Mill.

It was during this period when news came through

that Captain Jones had finally been given command of another ship. Also, he was to be commodore of a squadron which would sail in British waters on a cruise of destruction.

Banty Spooner said, "From what I heard, Dr. Franklin couldn't get Cap'n Jones much of a craft. She's an old merchantman, but I reckon John Paul Jones is mighty pleased with her. Anyway he's named her the *Bon Homme Richard* in honor of Ben Franklin's *Poor Richard*. About all he's worried about now, from what those new fellows who just arrived said, is getting himself a crew."

Jeremy's eyes glinted. "If only we could sign on with him."

Richard Dale smiled oddly. "Perhaps we will, Jeremy. We're nearly through with the tunnel."

Two days later Nat slipped into the tunnel to do his stint. He paused hearing an excited murmur ahead. Then: "Stop digging," Dale called in an urgent whisper. "Stop! We're through."

Someone jostled past Nat in the dark tunnel. "I saw a pinpoint of light where my stick poked through. Another few jabs and that hole will be big enough to let a man out."

"Back to the yard, men," Dale ordered. "Try not to look excited. Pass the word around to the others that we'll be going out tonight."

Later, in the prison house, the plotters did their best to appear nonchalant as they ate their supper in scattered groups. There was no need to huddle together for last-minute planning. Everything had been worked out in detail long, long since.

Israel Boone had been assigned to the task of over-powering the guard who would come to lock the prison house for the night. Once the man was bound and gagged, the prisoners would slink through the shadows and crawl into the tunnel. Emerging, they would break up into small parties and make their way to Plymouth, Southampton, and other coastal villages. They would be sheltered by sympathetic English people whose names and addresses had been secured by Dale. They would re-main hidden until passage to France could be arranged.

Jeremy, finishing his mug of weak tea, leaned close to Nat. "A few of the men," he said in a low tone, have decided not to go with us tonight, Nat. Asa Widgeon's one of them. He said that anyone who's caught will get the Black Hole. He thinks that at least half of us will be caught again."

"I had an idea he would back out," Nat said. "He'll wait to be exchanged."

"Calvin Crane isn't going out either."

"Calvin? Not going?" Nat was startled. "But——"

"He said he was needed here and he's right, Nat. Some here would die without his care. It wasn't an easy deci-sion for Calvin to make——"

Richard Dale stood up, an erect figure in the gloom. A sudden hush came over the prison. This was the signal.

A key was rattling in the lock of the door. The guard was there, locking up the prison house for the night. Israel Boone sprang from the shadows, his powerful arm encircling the guard's neck. Swiftly the guard was dragged inside, bound and gagged, and left in a dark cor-ner where he wouldn't be found until morning.

The men began filing out, melting silently into the darkness as they moved toward the tunnel entrance. Nat was among the last to go out. As he left the prison house with Jeremy and Dale, the latter locked the door with the key he had taken from the guard. He then put the key in his pocket.

They joined the silent cluster of prisoners at the tunnel entrance and waited there while the men crawled down into the hole one by one.

Presently Dick Dale whispered, "All right, Nat. In with you. Jeremy and I will be the last."

Nat was about to drop to his knees when he heard a voice come from the darkness, "Who's there. Is that you, guard?" Seth Cuffey!

The three prisoners froze. Ordinarily, Nat knew, Cuffey wouldn't appear in the yard without guards to protect him. But now he thought the prisoners were locked up. Perhaps he had got wind of the escape plot and had come to warn the guards.

Jeremy leaped, a dark shadow in the night. Nat heard the crunching sound of a vicious blow.

"Nice work, Jeremy," Dale whispered. "He's out cold. But we can't leave him here. Let me think a second or two———" He pondered, then: "We'll drag him into the tunnel and———" He thrust the key of the prison house into one of Cuffey's pockets. "We'll cave in that soft spot near the end of the tunnel and leave him there with only his head sticking out."

Jeremy chuckled softly. "And then it will look as if he was part of the plot and got himself trapped."

"Exactly. Go on ahead, Nat. Hurry."

Nat began crawling while behind him came Jeremy pulling and Dick Dale pushing Cuffey's heavy body through the narrow tunnel. After what seemed like half an eternity Nat caught a whiff of cool, sweet air. A moment or so later he heard Jeremy saying, "Lend a hand, Nat. Get some dirt over Cuffey——"

With the turncoat attended to, the three crawled out through the few remaining feet of the tunnel. They walked swiftly for a while and then Nat looked back. Old Mill was completely blanketed by the night.

"Don't look back, Nat," Jeremy said. He lifted an arm. "Look ahead, where we're going. Yonder's the Channel—and France. And the *Bon Homme Richard*."

CHAPTER TWENTY

HMS *Serapis,* Fifty Guns

THE ROTTING TIMBERS of the *Bon Homme Richard* creaked protestingly as the old vessel wallowed off the English east coast. She had made an almost complete circuit of the British Isles and now, with what was left of her squadron, was heading southeastward toward the Netherlands.

Nat Harkins was in the forecastle where the watch below was lounging about. Some were mending clothes. Others carved or read. Most, however, just talked. They chattered and argued continually in a half-dozen languages.

Snatches of French, Spanish, Italian, and Dutch reached Nat's ears. There were even some Malays among the deckhands. Until the prisoners from Old Mill had begun arriving in L'Orient and other French ports, Captain Jones had been hard put to find seamen willing to sail in the cranky old ship.

Nat thought about Old Mill as he applied his needle to a patch in a pair of britches. It seemed like only yesterday that he had crawled out of the tunnel with his companions. Yet nearly six months had passed since the escape. Six months—most of which had been spent on a cruise that seemed doomed to failure from the start.

Two bells sounded distantly, reminding Nat that it was time to relieve Jeremy on lookout duty. He put away his sewing kit in his seabag, donned his pea jacket, and went up the companionway. Dodging past some French marines who were drilling on deck, he jumped for the ratlines and clambered aloft.

Joining his brother in the crosstrees, Nat asked, "Any sign of that merchant fleet, Jeremy?"

He was referring to a large squadron of British merchant vessels, which, according to reports, was under way from Baltic seaports to England. The ships were said to be deep-laden with masts and various other materials urgently needed by the Royal Navy in its war with the United Colonies and France.

"Nary a sign, Nat."

Nat sighed. "If our bad luck holds, we'll miss that fleet. Or, if we do find it, I suppose it will have some big men-of-war for escorts."

"That won't worry Captain Jones," Jeremy said drily. "All that bothers him is the thought of finishing this cruise without doing any real fighting."

Nat nodded. "Some of the crew are calling this a hoodoo ship."

"Well, you know why, Nat. Captain Jones has had trouble for a shipmate ever since we shoved off. And most of it"—he scowled over the starboard bow at a trim man-of-war—"most of the trouble is due to the blithering idiot who commands that frigate."

Nat looked toward the *Alliance*, a fine frigate which

had been built only two years before in Massachusetts. Just why that fast, spic-and-span vessel had been turned over to an incompetent French captain like Pierre Landais, while Captain Jones had to be content with an ancient, lumbering old ex-merchantman, was a mystery to one and all aboard.

Sailing near the *Alliance* were the two remaining vessels in Captain Jones' squadron: the *Pallas,* a converted cargo ship, and the little *Vengeance,* a tender. Both were commanded by French captains.

Three other ships had sailed with the squadron from L'Orient, but their French captains, unwilling to take orders from Jones, had gone off on their own.

Still frowning at the *Alliance,* Jeremy went on, "You could search for years before you could find another such arrogant bufflehead and coward as Landais. The British admirals must love him."

Nat agreed. He was remembering what had happened almost immediately after the squadron set out from L'Orient. Captain Landais, deliberately disobeying signals, had rammed the *Bon Homme Richard.* The damage had forced both ships back to port where a month was required to make repairs.

Later, when Captain Jones was preparing to attack the town of Leith in Scotland, the *Alliance* suddenly vanished. The *Richard* waited for her but, by the time Landais put in an appearance, a storm had blown up and the raid had to be abandoned.

"You're right, Jeremy. Landais is more of a help to the British than to Captain Jones. With a little cooperation from the *Alliance* we'd have taken a lot more prizes than we have."

The storm had blown them far southward, and when it cleared, Nat glanced toward the shore. By now the English coast was so close that he could see the cattle in the fields. That bold cape, jutting pugnaciously seaward, would be Flamborough Head.

While the *Bon Homme Richard* stood past the cape and ran slowly southward, Nat darted a look below. Banty Spooner was at the wheel. Near him, pacing the high poopdeck, was the slender, erect figure of Captain Jones. Israel Boone was amidships with Richard Dale. Dale had been promoted from midshipman to lieutenant by the captain. The two were inspecting one of the cannon.

Nat knew full well that they were concerned over the guns, particularly the eighteen-pounders. Israel claimed that they had been condemned by the French Navy. He said they were old and might blow up with too heavy a charge. Still, they were all that Captain Jones could get. The French, having allied themselves with the United Colonies, were at war with England. Naturally they were concerned with arming their own ships first.

He shrugged. Probably the eighteen-pounders wouldn't be fired anyway. In a few days the squadron would reach a neutral port and the cruise would be over. Everything seemed to be against Captain Jones——

Abruptly Nat's musings came to an end. Suddenly he was staring at a patch of white sail looming ahead. When he made it out to be a small vessel he shouted, "Sail ho, starboard bow."

Crowding on canvas, the *Bon Homme Richard* went after the stranger which proved to be a small brigantine.

Just as a shot was about to be fired over her bows, Nat caught sight of another vessel standing southward past Flamborough Head. "Sail ho!" he cried again.

As if by magic another merchantman appeared. And another. "It's a fleet," he cried hoarsely as vessel after vessel came around the cape. He tried to count them but lost track. The ocean seemed to be filled with huge, square-rigged ships.

Captain Jones came aloft, followed by Lieutenant Dale. Leveling his glass, the captain declared, "That will be the Baltic fleet, Mr. Dale. At long-last fortune has favored us." The bare hint of a smile flitted across his grim features.

"They'll be escorted, sir," Dale reminded. "That one in the lead looks like a man-of-war to me, although no gunports are showing. The big square-rigger in the van looks like a frigate."

"Only two." Captain Jones' smile deepened. He leaned down, shouting an order to his signal officer. A few moments later colored signal flags shot up ordering the *Pallas*, *Vengeance*, and *Alliance* into battle formation. The *Pallas* and *Vengeance* obeyed the order and drew closer. The *Alliance*, however, came about and headed for the open sea.

"There goes Landais again," Lieutenant Dale said. "About to disappear when the fighting starts."

"I expected that," Captain Jones snapped. "I'm not depending on the *Alliance*."

The captain and lieutenant went below and presently Nat heard the drums roll out the beat to quarters.

As he began clambering down from the crosstrees,

Nat saw that the merchant fleet had begun to scatter in all directions like frightened chickens. The two men-of-war were in the midst of them, flying signals, trying desperately to bring them back into orderly formation.

By the time Nat reported to number four gun, a nine-pounder, the seamen were aloft, setting every inch of canvas. The French Marines were scrambling into the tops to man the swivels and taking positions elsewhere in the ship where they could subject the enemy to musket fire when the action began.

Israel Boone, in charge of the battery of nine-pounders, ordered the crews to bring up chain shot, powder, matches, and langrage: "On the double, lads."

Between trips below, Nat had an occasional glimpse of the enemy. The frightened merchant fleet had been partially reassembled and were coming about to head north past Flamborough Head. The two bulldogs now lay between the convoy they were protecting and Captain Jones' squadron.

The British warships, their yellow and black hulls glowing in the waning light, had been identified by crew members who had seen them in the past. The largest of the two was the *Serapis*, a new fifty-gun frigate commanded by a Captain Pearson. The other was the ship-of-war, *Countess of Scarborough*, twenty guns.

The sun dipped behind the white cliffs and a rosy glow tinted the sky. A bare whisper of a breeze blew the Colonial squadron ever closer to the two Britishers.

Israel growled, "Look at that *Alliance*. Standing off like she was a-feared of her own shadow."

One of the Frenchmen in the gun crew said bitterly,

"I am not proud of my countryman, Captain Landais. He is worse than stupid. He is a coward."

Although Captain Jones was continually signaling the *Alliance* to join the squadron, it was plain that he meant what he had said. He wasn't depending upon her for any assistance. Nor was he counting on help from the little *Vengeance* either. Unlike the *Pallas*, which was close by, the *Vengeance* was lagging far to the rear.

Just before darkness settled down, Nat glanced shoreward. Lining the crest of the chalk cliffs of Flamborough Head were hundreds of people. Without doubt they were English countrymen, gathered to watch the Royal Navy give the hated pirate, John Paul Jones, a proper thrashing.

Signal flags shot up in the *Bon Homme Richard* ordering the *Pallas* to engage the smaller of the British ships.

The word was passed. "Up gunports. Cast loose the guns!"

Nat's heart pounded. His spine tingled as the gunports creaked and the guns were hauled back for loading. Slow matches glowed weirdly in the darkness as the *Richard* crept closer to the British frigate.

Someone whispered, "There she be," and a dark hulk loomed dead ahead.

The silence continued as the moon rose, a golden ball in the clear starry night.

Suddenly, a deep voice resounded over the sea from the deck of the *Serapis*:

"What ship is that?"

CHAPTER TWENTY-ONE

The Iron Captain

CAPTAIN JONES did not reply to the hail from the Serapis. He was biding his time, hoping to surprise the enemy with a damaging broadside.

The British captain shouted again, "What ship is that? Answer or I'll fire!"

The *Bon Homme Richard* ran on, straight as an arrow toward the powerful frigate. She was almost upon the *Serapis* when she swerved and the order came:

"Commence firing."

Flame and thunder burst upon the night as both ships unleashed raking broadsides at point-blank range. The *Richard's* decks shook so violently under the impact that Nat could hardly stay on his feet. Staggering to the shot rack, he could hear the sharp, staccato barking of the swivels in the tops. Hoarse cries of pain mingled with the crash of falling spars.

A solid ribbon of flame belched from the *Serapis* as her lower tier of heavy guns went into action and blasted the *Richard*. As the vessel shuddered, Israel shouted, "Swab, load, you lubbers!"

205

A blinding sheet of flame blossomed aft on the *Richard* together with a deafening explosion. Moments later a hoarse voice yelled, "The eighteen-pounders. Two of 'em blew up and killed most of their crews."

The battle continued in the moonlight, with both vessels mauling each other with broadside after broadside. The *Richard's* decks were aslant, which meant she was taking water. Her rigging and sails were being shot away by the British gunners. Nat wondered how long she could remain afloat.

During a brief, odd sort of lull in the welter of confused, crashing sounds, Nat heard panic-stricken cries from below. "The prisoners in the hold," Israel Boone rumbled. "Reckon they're a-feared they'll be trapped if we sink." He took a slow match from the tub. "Can't say as I blame 'em. That frigate is throwin' plenty of metal at us."

Gaping holes riddled the *Richard's* hull. She was on fire in many places on deck and below. One by one her cannon were silenced. Some had blown up, killing most of the gunners. Others were shattered by the enemy's big guns. A few nine-pounders were all that were left in action.

One of the French sailors, working alongside Nat, said in broken English, "We are defeat. Why does not Captain Jones surrender?"

And why didn't Captain Jones surrender, Nat wondered. With the *Richard* sinking, with most of her guns out of action and half of her crew dead or wounded, her commander could never be blamed for striking his colors. Yet, instead of surrendering, Captain Jones was shouting orders that would bring his ship even closer to the enemy.

The moments that followed were only a confused blur to Nat. He served the gun with Israel's crew until it was shattered by a shot from the *Serapis*. After that he found himself below, with Jeremy and Israel, helping to man the pumps or passing buckets of sea water to put out the many fires. When he came back on deck again, stumbling over limp figures, he saw that the two ships were locked together. The *Serapis* bowsprit was lashed fast to the *Richard's* mizzenmast.

Vaguely Nat wondered why a boarding party from the enemy wasn't streaming aboard the *Richard*. The crackle of musketry from aloft gave him the answer. The *Richard's* sharpshooters and marines were at work, popping away at any head which appeared on the enemy's decks. The *Serapis* cannon, however, continued to pour their salvos into the *Richard*.

Captain Jones dashed forward through a shroud of smoke with Lieutenant Dale. "Come on, lads," he snapped. "Lend a hand getting that nine-pounder to starboard adrift. Haul it to larboard and put it to work."

They unlashed the cannon. As they were rolling it across the tilting deck to larboard, Jeremy cried, "The *Alliance*. Here come the *Alliance!*"

A hoarse cheer rose. If the *Alliance* lent a hand, they would have a chance.

The *Alliance* stood in closer. She came around the *Richard's* stern, her batteries belching smoke and flame.

Men fell on the *Richard*. Shocked, furious curses were flung at the French captain who, instead of firing at the enemy, had raked the *Richard* with a broadside.

"You blasted fool!" Banty Spooner shrilled.

"Fool!" Nat repeated hollowly. It didn't seem possible that Landais could make such a mistake. Both vessels were plainly visible in the moonlight. The British vessel was black with a yellow stripe. The *Richard* was jet black. Yet the Frenchman had erred.

The *Alliance* came around and ran past the *Richard* again, and once more a murderous salvo of langrage and chain shot mowed down a cluster of seamen in the waist.

Then, abruptly, the *Alliance* headed for the open sea. It seemed to Nat that Captain Landais must have realized his awful blunder and then, losing his wits entirely, could decide on no other course than fleeing from the scene of battle.

There was no time now, though, to speculate about the *Alliance*. The nine-pounder had to be set up to bear upon the enemy. The gun was hardly in place when a seaman came dashing aft shouting, "The prisoners are out! The sailin' master turned 'em loose——"

Nat whirled. The prisoners, over a hundred of them, were streaming onto the deck, making a desperate effort to go aboard the *Serapis*.

Lieutenant Dale dashed forward, shouting at the prisoners. "Below, every last man. Below and man the pumps or we'll all be in Davy Jones' Locker."

"Come on, lads," Israel rumbled. "Let's us give Dick a hand." He strode toward the prisoners, cutlass swinging. Behind him came Banty Spooner, Jeremy, and Nat. Steel flashed in the moonlight. The prisoners hesitated, then suddenly turned and filed below.

Now Dick Dale was shouting, "Get that nine-pounder into action, boys, or it'll be back to Old Mill for the lot of us."

A seaman near Nat muttered, "We'll never see Old Mill. We'll all be dead before much longer."

The *Richard* was a mass of flames as fire ate into her. Probably, Nat was thinking, the only reason she was still afloat was because she was lashed to the *Serapis*. Only two nine-pounders remained in action. How long could Captain Jones hold out?

The answer came quickly. One of the gunners and the carpenter came stumbling aft. Both men were badly wounded and their faces were contorted with agony. Running to the bulwarks they screamed to the British captain, "Quarter, sir. Give us quarter."

Captain Pearson of the *Serapis* heard them. Ordering his gunners to cease firing, he shouted to the captain of the *Bon Homme Richard*.

Have you struck, sir?"

The answer was given in words that Nat would never forget as long as he lived.

"Struck, sir?" John Paul Jones' deep clear voice resounded over the moonlit sea. "No! I have just begun to fight!"

Nat squared his shoulders. All the weariness and sense of defeat left him as he ran to the shot rack.

Then, the brief lull over, the guns of the *Serapis* went

into action again, and her thundering salvos were answered by the puny nine-pounders of the *Richard*. But to Nat the battle was no longer hopeless. He kept repeating to himself, "We have just begun to fight——"

Aloft, a seaman had courageously followed an order to go out onto the *Richard's* main yard which swung over the deck of the *Serapis*. He carried a leather pail filled with hand grenades which he began tossing into an open hatch. Two grenades exploded on the deck of the Britisher, but the third disappeared into the vitals of the big frigate. A shattering explosion followed, and hoarse cries of panic came from the enemy vessel.

"Boarders," Captain Jones was shouting. "Boarders. Away, boarders."

The *Richard's* men needed no urging. They swarmed over the bulwarks and onto the deck of the *Serapis*, cutlasses gleaming.

Then, as suddenly as it had begun, the battle ended. Captain Pearson of the *Serapis* was hauling down his colors!

The guns were silent. A peculiar hush fell over both ships. As the British emblem fell in a crumpled pile on the deck, Israel Boone said in a husky whisper, "We're sinking, Nat. The *Richard* is sinking. We'll have to cut her loose and let her go." He took a long breath. "Reckon we won't ever see anything like this again. A bulldog captain striking his colors to an enemy ship he's all but sent to the bottom."

But the *Richard* was still afloat when Captain Pearson of the *Serapis* stepped aboard her, where he unbuckled his sword and handed it gravely to Captain John Paul Jones.

Captain Pearson had surrendered—but not to a ship which he had battered to pieces. He had surrendered to a man who would never admit defeat.

CHAPTER TWENTY-TWO

The *True American,* Privateer

THE TEMPTING FRAGRANCE of baked beans and corn bread filled Abigail Harkins' kitchen in Boston. As she set the table she hummed the melody of "Yankee Doodle." Now and then she glanced fondly at Nat, who was at the hearth reading the Boston *Gazette*.

Heavens to Betsy, she thought, how that boy has grown. Taller right now than his father ever had been. She'd hardly known Nat when he came home from France with Jeremy aboard the *Ariel* commanded by that Captain Jones.

He was still too skinny though. No matter. She'd put meat on his bones now that he was home. And perhaps he'd stay home, too, now that he realized how important it was to build ships.

As for Jeremy—she shook her head. He was chafing to be off again. She had a notion that the reason he'd gone off to Beverly with Israel and Banty Spooner was to look over some ship or other. If they found a suitable craft, Boston couldn't hold them for long.

What was keeping them, she wondered. They had promised to be back in time for supper tonight and here it was well after sundown.

Nat put the paper down and stared into the fire.

"More bad news, Nat?" she asked.

Nat nodded. The patriots were suffering one defeat after another in the southern colonies. General Washington's army was still camped in New Jersey, their spirits at low ebb. Not even the arrival of six thousand French troops had rallied them.

At sea the situation was almost as alarming. Most of the thirteen fine new frigates built for the Colonial navy were gone. Some had been lost in sea battles; others were being burned in the ports where they were built so that they wouldn't fall into British hands.

But most discouraging to Nat was the way Captain John Paul Jones was being treated by Congress.

"After all he's done, Aunty," he said bitterly, "the Marine Committee is charging him with holding up French military supplies. The papers says there's even talk about investigating Benjamin Franklin for the same reason."

"Politicians," Aunt Abigail snapped. "Someday, Nat, you'll realize that there are always a few buffleheads among them trying to bring bigger men than they are down to their own size. There's some in Congress who hate Ben Franklin and——"

Footsteps sounded outside and the door swung open to admit Jeremy, Israel, and Banty Spooner.

"Victuals," exclaimed Banty, sniffing. "How long before supper will be ready?"

Israel grinned. "Banty, you've got the appetite of a sea gull."

"Wash up, all of you," Aunt Abigail ordered. "Then set down. Everything's ready."

When supper was served, Israel said, "Well Nat, we found ourselves a ship today. She's a brig called the *True American* and by golly she'll sail circles around anything that floats."

"She's a trim craft, Nat," Jeremy said, his eyes gleaming. "Banty will be skipper. Israel is sailing as mate and I'll be second. We could use another officer." He gave Nat a quick glance.

"Now, now, Jeremy," Aunt Abigail said. "Nat wants to build ships and you know how important that is———"

Someone rapped on the door and Nat ran to open it.

"Asa!" he exclaimed. "Asa Widgeon."

The others rose to surround the sailing master, firing questions at him.

"I just got into Boston," Asa Widgeon explained. "I stopped by the Blue Dragon and Caleb Wickerby told me I'd find you fellers here, so———"

"Don't tell us you slipped out of Old Mill," Israel asked.

"No, I was exchanged," Asa said. "Quite a lot of us got out that way. According to the talk on that privateer I came over in from France, Dr. Franklin was able to fix up exchanging because that Captain Jones took so many British sailors when he was cruising around over there."

Nat presented the sailing master to his aunt, who said, "Set down, Mr. Widgeon, there's plenty for all."

"Reckon I will, ma'am," Asa said eagerly. "Shoreside victuals will be a treat for me."

Asa dove into the beans and corn bread, answering questions between mouthfuls.

"Aye, Nat, Calvin Crane's still in Old Mill. When I left he was mighty busy doctoring Cap'n Beeler, Reddy Malone, Duff, and some of our other shipmates from the *Dauntless*. The British claimed their hospitals were full and so they booted them all into the prison. They're doing fine under Calvin's care. They'll all be exchanged before long."

"What about that polecat, Seth Cuffey?" Israel asked.

"Him? The guards found him trapped in that tunnel, and so they reckoned he was in on the plot."

"And did he manage to talk himself out of it?"

"He almost did at that. Had 'em about convinced, I heard, until they found the prison house key in his pocket. He got the Black Hole. Sixty days. He was still in it when I got out." Asa helped himself to more beans, then: "I heard from Caleb that you fellers aim to go privateering again. That right?"

"That we are, Asa," Banty said. "Fact is we got a fine brig, the *True American*. We'll sail soon as we can round up a crew."

"Well," Asa put down his knife and fork. "I hope you're not counting on me to go along as sailin' master. No point in fighting any more far as I can see. We haven't got a chance against the British. Our navy's been shot off the sea. As for the army, I hear men are deserting General Washington by the hundreds."

"Thousands of others are staying with him," Jeremy said quietly.

Asa shrugged. "It's a hopeless fight, so we might just as well get it through our heads that Britain is a powerful nation and she's got the biggest navy in the world. We got nothing to fight with so——"

"Nothing?" Aunt Abigail had pushed back her chair. Rising, she shook a finger under Asa Widgeon's nose. "What did that Captain John Paul Jones have when he licked that frigate called the *Serapis*?"

"Well, now, I wasn't in that fight myself, so——"

"Well, I was," Jeremy said sharply, "and by Jupiter I'll tell you about it, Asa——" He went on and in angry words described the fight between the *Serapis* and the *Bon Homme Richard*.

Nat's pulse beat faster as he listened. Once again he was aboard the battered, sinking ship, her decks strewn with dead and her little cannon replying to the mighty salvos from the *Serapis*. Once more he heard the British captain's words: "Have you struck, sir?" and the defiant answer, "No! I have just begun to fight."

When Jeremy finished, Aunt Abigail said, "So now you see, Mr. Widgeon, that, like Captain Jones, these colonies have just begun to fight, and if you had any gumption at all, you'd be doing the same thing."

"Well, ma'am," Asa said hesitantly, "since you put it like that, I reckon we ought to keep on for a spell yet. I'll sign with you fellers in the *True American* if you'll have me."

"And you, Nat?" Jeremy asked.

Aunt Abigail looked at Nat. The answer was there in his eyes as she knew it would be. She rose and turned away, dabbing her eyes with her apron. It wouldn't do to let them see the tears.